MOONLIGHT OVER PEARL | TEN STORIES FROM ASPEN

Moonlight Over Pearl

Ten Stories from Aspen

PAUL ANDERSEN

ROARING FORK PRESS | ASPEN, COLORADO

DEDICATION

This book is dedicated to Lu Krueger-Andersen, my wife of eighteen years, who has always encouraged and believed in my writing, often more than I have. A free-lance writer's greatest support—practically and personally—comes from a working spouse. I couldn't have written this book without her unflagging encouragement.

ILLUSTRATION & DESIGN BY CURT CARPENTER

ROARING FORK PRESS
Post Office Box 2047 | Basalt, Colorado 81621
andersen@rof.net

ISBN 978-0-615-33158-4

PRINTED IN THE UNITED STATES

Contents

Acknowledgments

I N 1984, I rode my mountain bike over Taylor Pass from Crested Butte to Aspen for a job interview at the *Aspen Times*. To my delight, Bil Dunaway and Mary Eshbaugh Hayes made a leap of faith and hired me on the spot. Mary, as editor, inspired me to explore every facet of Aspen through my job as a reporter. Bil, as publisher, gave me enough latitude to pursue anything that caught my interest. Over the ensuing decade, the *Aspen Times* provided an incredible education and enriching life experience.

I am indebted to my friends, those with whom I have skied, hiked, biked, climbed and shared the exuberance for life and the incredible passion for nature we have discovered and built upon over the course of many memorable outdoor adventures.

The Aspen Institute has been a vital part of my inspiration for exploring the world of ideas through seminars I've both moderated and attended. The Institute has changed dramatically since Walter Paepcke's time, but the virtues of his lofty, original vision for body/mind/spirit remain for those who seek them.

Aspen's many historians, authors and archivists have helped form my view of Aspen's deep history, from which I've drawn a sense of wonder for the original wilderness and respect for the pioneers who came into that wilderness. The scope of history is alive and well in Aspen, in part because it is heroic, and in part because it is so very recent.

To those who have read these stories and worked with me on content, historical accuracy, style, and myriad editorial details, I'm in your debt. Chief among you are Hensley Peterson, Carol Bayley, and Lu Krueger-Andersen. My gratitude for making this book also goes to Curt Carpenter, a great designer, illustrator and book publishing partner.

Finally, to the many and unforgettable people and places of Aspen, which have provided both actors and stage for human drama amid natural wonders, I am deeply grateful for having lived among you. ☆

Preface

P AUL ANDERSEN knows Aspen—and that's more of an achievement than it might seem.

Aspen is, of course—as "everyone" knows—a glitzy, international ski resort, a town where the billionaires have pushed out the mere millionaires. It is also, of course, a beautiful, historic town nestled at the top of an extraordinary Rocky Mountain valley.

But the real Aspen (and I blush to use that phrase, but use it nonetheless) is more than that—much more. And Paul Andersen knows first-hand so many of Aspen's faces.

Paul knows the Aspen that is home to true mountaineers, alpine adventurers who put themselves at mortal risk to get close to the reality of life itself. He also knows the overlapping group of hard-core mountain crazies, who may not dream of conquering Everest, but who push their personal limits relentlessly, just for the sheer hell of it.

And he knows well how these mountain adventures can turn in an instant to life and death drama.

But, tellingly, Paul also knows the Aspen that is home to the Aspen Music Festival. He paints this aspect of Aspen with real feeling and emotional depth—with understanding of the truer stakes of the artistic life—in one magnificent story.

And then, again, his focus can encompass the intellectual side of Aspen on display at the executive seminars of the Aspen Institute, in which minds, assumptions and lives are challenged—and may or may not actually change.

And more...Paul touches on the Aspen of the intellectual "ski bum," a once-gloried but now fading part of Aspen. And he finds time and space for Aspen's frontier roots, the "Wild West" of the miners and explorers who settled the Roaring Fork Valley.

In these ten stories, Paul Andersen has explored and revealed so much of Aspen—and done it so well—and somehow managed to do it without ever touching on the "glitz," the glamour, or the billionaires.

Paul's stories are tied together by the thread of Walter Paepcke's "Aspen Idea," the town as a unique place to sustain the body, mind and spirit. That thread runs through these stories.

But, even more, these ten fine stories are an exploration of Aspen's character, defined by a sense of adventure and daring that includes a willingness to face failure and even death. It's a wonderfully written portrait of an extraordinary town over the course of more than a century. And it makes me proud, yet again, to call Aspen home. ☆

—ANDY STONE, former editor of the *Aspen Times*

Introduction

KATHRYN THALBERG, the late founder of Explore Booksellers and a person of letters, told me twenty years ago that the definitive book about Aspen had yet to be written. Kathryn was right. In fact, no single book, no matter how comprehensive, will ever encompass all of Aspen. For that, dozens of books must be written, and they have. Aspen's impressive bibliography represents a diverse and fascinating study.

As an Aspen writer since 1984, my interests have been across the board—history, culture, art, politics, environment, business, society, nature, and mountaineering. The more I learn, the more fascinating are the many influences that have woven Aspen's colorful social fabric. If Aspen had a genome, it would be a complex set of codes influencing an ever evolving organism. This book offers one more exploration of that complex organism.

The settings and experiences described herein come from personal experiences, many of them first written in journalistic form for the *Aspen Times*, where I was a reporter for ten years (1984-1993) and where I continue to write a weekly column. Some stories in this book originate from feature articles I have free-lanced for local magazines, or they reflect my preoccupation with the "Aspen Idea" and the core philosophic values of Aspen's renaissance in 1949.

I have self-published these stories as an act of faith, believing that they are valid interpretations of the Aspen I have come to know. My hope is that this book will add another dimension to the literary expression of a unique community from which I have derived memorable experiences. ☆

—PAUL ANDERSEN

Chapter 1 | Black Ice

"ERIK! MONITOR LAKE! BLACK ICE!" Avery leaves a voicemail on a cold December morning. "New plate...big as a footfall field. You need to get over here, buddy. Can you bust a move?"

For Erik there is no doubt. He breaks a date with his girlfriend, puts off a client whose software installation can wait. Nothing else matters. Black ice is now.

It's good to be on the road in the old Volvo, the defroster cranked up against the icy cold. Vintage rock blasts from crackling speakers. Skating gear takes up the back seat, along with a folding lawn chair. A cooler with food and beer occupies the passenger seat.

The highway snakes down the valley and snowy peaks fill Erik's rear view mirror. He turns onto a two-lane road that meanders up another valley toward another range of snowy peaks. The old car labors up and over a mountain pass where the sun strobes through sunlit aspen groves. The road curves along a river choked with ice, the air clouded with steam. Frost flocks the willows white. He navigates patches of ice and snow, slows through a sleepy ranch town where a pickup idles in front of the cafe. The old Volvo grinds up the long switchback to the mesa where the sky opens and a golden eagle soars and hoof prints puncture the shallow crust of snow that's dotted with sage. With the sun low and glinting through a crack in his windshield, Erik reaches Monitor Lake.

He pulls up and blasts his high-pitched horn. He gives high fives, then hurriedly unloads his cooler, lawn chair, rope, hand-picks and life jacket. Someone asks if Erik has brought his wooden shoes. They make light of Erik's Dutch origins, but respect his devotion to skating, his cultural identity. Some already have their skates on and are making gradually expanding loops onto the lake.

Erik is drawn to the edge. He crouches down, pulls off his gloves, and spreads out his fingers. He presses his hands against the hard coldness and reads the ice, its brief history told in crystalline veins where captured air bubbles are beaded up like mercury. The ice stretches like plate steel in a huge sheet with perfect uniformity. It absorbs sunlight the way a black hole sucks up the sun.

Someone passes a joint. Avery tells a story about skating on Humboldt Lake the weekend before with Penrose. "Why isn't Penrose here?" demands Erik. "Fuckin' the dog," quips Avery. "What about Andy?" "Home with the wife and kids." Meanwhile, they are pushing feet into skate boots, adjusting lace tension, blowing on fingertips.

Erik pulls on his gloves and tugs his hat down over his numbing ears. His skates are snug and comfortable, his feet cool. He needs to move, too anxious to bother with the tools of survival—hand picks, the length of rope, the life jacket. He needs a quick warm-up, a quick blast across the ice.

Erik totters down to the gravelly shore and pulls off his skate guards. He steps onto the ice and smoothly embraces his old love, a love he's known since childhood when he learned to skate the frozen canals of Utrecht. He'll return for the gear when the serious skating begins, when he and Avery will distance themselves from the others in search of the perfect plate. It was years ago on skates that their friendship formed and solidified. It happened the way water freezes, transforming something fluid into something solid. Warm friends on cold ice.

Erik's sharp blades score the uniform surface. Razor-thin contact imparts the deepest grace Erik knows. He feels the bite of his inside edge, riding it with perfect balance in a tightening arc. He leaves the shore where Avery is still hunched over in his lawn chair, lacing. Erik breathes deeply, feeling the coldness burn in his throat. There is stiffness in his legs from the long drive. He stretches as he skates, feeling the pliant resilience of muscles, tendons, ligaments. The blood moves through his veins, pumping through his heart with radiant heat.

Each thrust carries him faster along the shoreline. There is a twinge of pain in his left knee, the ski injury that never heals. He keeps skating, smoothly, easily, in a relaxed cadence that is as natural to him as walking, perhaps more natural. He shifts from skate to skate with the balance and rhythm of a dancer. A reggae tune fills his head and he works it for tempo. The beat helps him blot out the distractions that have been plaguing him—the plebian details of life. He finds a smooth place inside himself, as quiet as the mountain air. His soul lives in this place.

The voices of the others fade in the distance as Erik leans low from the waist, his hips and knees working, his arms swinging with pendulum regularity. His skates sing. He increases his tempo for a five-stroke sprint that leaves him flying and winded. The air burns his cheeks. His eyes water behind wraparound sunglasses. The tears freeze into diamonds on his beard. He leans forward, pulls his skates together, and rests his hands on his thighs. With gentle angulations he shifts from side to side. Twin grooves meander in serpentine, symmetrical perfection; his signature written in Hans Brinker graffiti.

Erik comes to a stop and stretches tall, taking in his surroundings. He listens to the comforting silence of the lake and the country beyond. The winter sun glances over snow-covered hills that rise beyond the shore. At the blue-hazed horizon are distant mountains capped by pale, lenticular ice clouds shaped like berets. The sky is woven with jet contrails. He flexes his knees and feels a vibration through his skates. The ice is alive, shifting, dynamic. He is suddenly euphoric.

He gazes down between his skates into three inches of sun-sparkled purity. He stabs with the heel of his right skate and produces a chip. He reaches down, pinches it between his gloved fingers, and studies it against the light, like a jeweler examining a gem stone. He pops it into his mouth and it stings his tongue with a slight bitterness. He takes in the curvaceous waterline where the lake has yet to freeze. Steam rises in soft whirls over metallic gray water. A gentle curve reveals where a fresh plate of ice juts in a narrow peninsula onto the open water.

He looks back. Avery is on the ice, beckoning to Erik with a sweep of his gloved hand. Erik watches his friend lower his head and begin skating fast and hard, his hands swinging, his fingertips almost touching the surface. Erik's legs can no longer be still. He pushes off with a shaving of fine crystals. In five strokes he is cruising at top speed, his long shadow bent in a low crouch.

Erik reaches the mouth of the fresh plate and slows his tempo. He turns and sees his friend, now in full stride, his rhythm strong, the swing of his legs and arms perfectly coordinated. Erik studies the motion and exults in the magic of a man gliding over a floating plate of ice. He notices that the others have pushed off and are skating the opposite way around the lake.

As Avery closes in fast, Erik cannot keep still. His adrenaline overpowers his caution and he pushes off for the new peninsula. He studies the ice as he goes and sees its complexion change by the deepening of its hue. Soon the ice is jet black. Few air bubbles mar its composition. Erik knows it was formed less than twenty-four hours ago in the deep freeze of the sub-zero night.

He is intoxicated by the impossibly smooth plate. He wants it first, before anyone else, even his best friend. Erik is suddenly skating for all of Holland, for his forebears, for his national pride. His legs are untiring and powerful. He wants to shout his joy for his distant countrymen to hear. Before he knows it, he is more than halfway out onto the peninsula. He feels as if he could skate across the open water, a swan alighting on spreading wings.

A sudden vibration shatters Erik's composure, a booming sensation, felt more than heard. The ice speaks subtly, quietly, but with absolute authority. It is the voice of glaciers and ice ages issuing a grave warning that electrifies his senses. Erik glances down. His heart skips a beat and he sucks in a sharp breath. The ice is no longer uniform. There are imperfections in the plate. He has crossed a tangible line in those imperfections.

Erik spreads his legs to distribute his weight. He slows and turns. He studies his tracks where they crossed a pale meandering weakness bisecting the peninsula. Water oozes from fractures and spreads in a glossy film that obliterates his tracks. There is a jagged fracture across the narrow neck of the peninsula. Erik's heart beats fast and heat prickles his scalp.

"Hey Ho, Erik!" shouts Avery, who stops half way out on the peninsula. There is caution in his voice, masked by chiding. "Erik! I hope you're not going for a swim. You forgot your Speedo!"

Erik notices with deep misgivings that Avery, following Erik's lead, is empty handed—no rope, no life jacket, no picks. The weak swath of ice lies between them, a formidable boundary. Avery skates slowly toward Erik, whose mind rings an alarm. "No! Don't come out! There's a fracture!"

Erik realizes he was lucky to cross the weakness dividing the plates without going in, that the tensile strength of ice and water miraculously withstood his weight. He approaches it now, tentatively. The gap between the plates has widened to half an inch. The plate on which he stands is slowly separating from the main plate.

"Can you cross back?" shouts Avery.

"I don't know! And me without my fucking PFD!"

Avery holds up his hands. "Stay there. I'll get the gear. Is it solid enough?"

Erik studies the ice. His heart races as he realizes he's never been on anything so thin. Three-quarters...half an inch? He has seen people skating half an inch, but not without a PFD. Fear grips him. He feels like a fool. He back skates away from the expanding fissure.

"Go! And hurry!" he shouts. Avery turns and skates off at top speed.

Erik's body is tense. A cramp grips the toes of his right foot, curling them under. He shifts his weight onto the cramping foot, pressing his rebellious toes flat. With that subtle motion he feels a shift in the ice, a faint ripple. He quickly reapportions his weight to both skates. But something slow and methodical is underway, a dynamic that began with the tremor of Erik's first crossing. The equilibrium of the ice has been disturbed, its strength compromised. The plate is frail, like the shell of a bird's egg. Bonds are breaking.

"Hey, wait!" Erik's voice carries over the ice. Avery, a hundred yards away, wheels in a fast turn.

Erik stands, legs apart, hoping the sickening undulations will stop, that the upheavals will calm. But the thin plate can no longer hold his weight; it sags and disintegrates. Erik feels his skates breaking through. The surface cracks around him. With a gasp, Erik slips through a ragged hole in the plate and plunges beneath the surface.

He strokes hard and resurfaces. He gasps for breath. The cold air burns in his throat and the frigid water grips his body. Adrenaline courses through him. He kicks hard and paws his way through ice chunks, desperate to reach something solid. The thin ice shears with every lurching, clawing thrust he makes. Realizing the futility of the struggle, he reaches out with his arms, carefully levering his weight over the ice. The plate holds him. He gasps from the paralyzing cold of the water that has soaked through his clothes. Panic seizes him and he makes another desperate effort, kicking and clawing to get out. His sodden gloves are slippery so he flings them off. He digs his fingernails into the breaking ice. The plate fractures and he plunges back beneath the water.

Erik comes up sputtering for air, sobered by the icy dunking. He kicks hard and strokes toward the broken edge. He stretches out his arms onto the plate and kicks steadily for stability. The plate holds. He fixes his gaze on Avery, who skates cautiously back onto the peninsula. Erik can see his friend's shocked expression. What he cannot see is the violent trembling that shakes Avery to his core. Avery skates toward him.

"Don't try it!" cautions Erik. "It's too weak."

Avery ignores him. He studies the gap in the plates that has now grown to six inches. "I think I can cross."

"No! Then we'll both be stuck. Go back!" Erik feels the drag and pull of his clothing. The water tugs on him with a strengthening grip. It is freezing his body, stealing his warmth. His skates, which have always been his wings, are pulling him down.

"The rope!" Erik shouts. "That's the only way!"

This time Avery listens.

"Can you hang on that long?"

"Fuck if I know."

"That's not good enough. I'm coming for you!"

"No!" cries Erik. "Don't be stupid!"

"Look who's stupid!"

Erik watches Avery skate this way and that, searching for a crossing. Avery retreats, and Erik thinks he is going for the rope. Erik knows there can be no other help than Avery. The numbness will soon take his strength and the water will finish him. He watches his friend slowly skate away, but wonders why he is skating so slowly.

Avery stops and turns, pauses, then sprints toward Erik. From his position, low on the ice, Erik can see a smooth undulation rising on the thin ice. The plate bulges in a wave before Avery's oncoming skates. When Avery reaches the line of weakness between the plates he makes a fast skip, stretching his left leg far ahead of the right. Erik holds his breath. Avery lands on the plate. His skate blade cracks through, but he jerks it free with a running motion. With acrobatic skill, Avery launches his body forward in a graceful swan dive, catching his weight on his outstretched arms and legs, sliding forward in the form of a sky diver.

It appears that Avery will skid into the hole where Erik treads water, but he stops short. A wave of icy water pushed forward by Avery's body sloshes across the ice and spills over Erik's hands and arms. Erik and Avery stare at each other from a vantage point just inches above the ice. Avery suddenly smiles.

"So, you decided to take a bath today, Erik. But you didn't bring the soap?"

Erik smiles, but lacks a rejoinder. His focus is on pumping his tingling legs. His fingers are numb and cramped like claws. His fingernails are blue where they dig into the ice. Erik watches Avery scoot forward, inch by inch. Erik begins to pray. Perhaps the Christian God he has so willfully ignored all his agnostic life will recognize his voice. Perhaps there is forgiveness and mercy. "Dear God. Dear God. Dear God...please!"

Avery moves closer. He looks absurdly crab like. Erik can hear him breathing in short gasps. Avery is being ridiculously methodical, and Erik wearies of the waiting. He tries to boost himself forward with a kick and a lurch. The plate bends with elasticity.

"Don't move! Hold tight!" commands Avery, a desperate edge to his voice. "Be patient."

"I messed up, buddy," confesses Erik. "Just don't go in, or we're both done."

"I can't just leave you here! That's not part of the plan."

Avery inches forward until he touches Erik's fingertips. Erik can see the gloved hands touch his fingers, but he feels nothing. Avery then does something Erik thinks strange. He carefully swivels his body in a circle until his skates are inches from Erik's hands.

"Can you grip my blades? Can you climb out by holding onto me?"

Erik lifts his right arm, but it causes him to slip further into the water. He slaps his hand back onto the ice, feeling its numb weight.

"My hands are gone," says Erik. "I can't feel 'em." A wave of cold runs through him and his teeth clench in a spasm.

"Okay...okay. Hang on. Just hang on."

Avery carefully rolls over onto his back, then slowly sits up, spreading his legs out before him. Avery pulls off his gloves and inches toward Erik. He leans forward, reaching between his legs. He grasps Erik's wrists. Erik can feel the pressure of Avery's hands. He kicks from memory, moving the dead weights of his legs in a jerking rhythm.

"Okay, buddy, you're coming with me."

Avery's lips compress into a thin line as he tightens his grip on Erik's wrists. Avery's eyes are dark and focused. Erik has never realized the intensity of those eyes, and he marvels at their life force. He locks his gaze on them.

Avery angles the blades of his skates against the ice and begins to pull. Erik feels the slow, powerful force as his chest moves up and onto the ice. He begins to hope. He and Avery will skate away from this. It will become a memory, something to recount in later years, a legend of sorts. Suddenly, Avery's left skate blade loses its edge and skitters on the ice. Avery twists precariously toward the hole and releases his grip. Erik slips slowly back into the water, his chin just above the surface, his arms spread out on the ice. His hope dies, a light that suddenly goes dark.

"Shit!" says Avery, breathing fast and short. "Next time I pull, you've got to kick hard, okay?"

"My legs are numb," sighs Erik. "They're dead."

"You've gotta try, Erik! Now get ready."

Avery squares himself again to the hole, his legs outstretched. This time, he delicately taps with his long skates until both heel blades are embedded like spikes. Avery is anchored. "Okay, buddy, when I pull, you straighten your legs so I can slide you out. Then I'm going to move back and pull again. You understand?"

The meaning of Avery's words is elusive, a flimsy thread that's difficult for Erik to grasp. He's tired and cold and disoriented, but he keeps his eyes locked on Avery's, fixating on their intensity. "Okay," he nods.

Avery grips Erik's wrists and begins to pull. Erik feels his arms stretch as Avery extends his legs. Erik is dragged two feet out of the hole. He lies face down on the ice between Avery's legs. He must twist his head sideways to breathe. He gasps in spasms, jolted by violent shivers, his teeth clattering.

"I have to let go for a moment," warns Avery, releasing his grip.

Erik's torso settles onto the ice while his legs remain in the water. His saturated clothing stiffens in the frigid cold. He hears the tap, tap, tap of skate blades as Avery sets his anchors.

"Okay, buddy. This time, straighten your legs."

Erik's legs are logs in the slushy water. He can hardly move them.

"On three. One...two...three!"

Erik feels the pressure on his arms. He arches his back. In a smooth, birth-like motion, he is delivered from the water. He lies on the ice like the prize catch of an ice fisherman. The pressure on Erik's wrists eases.

Avery gasps for air. "Fuck, man! We did it."

Erik is stiff with cold, deeply exhausted. His mind is confused. He can't focus his thoughts.

"Erik! Erik! Do you hear me?"

Erik tries to prop up his head, but something keeps him down.

"Don't move!" says Avery. "I've got to figure out the best way from here."

Erik lies still while Avery scrabbles about. An eternity passes. His ear pressed to the ice, Erik can hear a faint tinkling as the water freezes around him, the crystals chaining together into facets, the facets joining into planes, the planes forming into plates.

Suddenly, Avery's face slides in line with Erik's. Avery, spread eagle on the ice, has come back. What Avery sees alarms him; Erik's face is white, his lips blue, his eyes dim. What Erik sees relieves him; the reassuring smile, the intense eyes, his friend so near.

"Erik, can you move?"

Erik blinks his eyes. He has no voice.

"Can you crawl?"

Erik studies his friend's face with detached curiosity, trying to fathom what it means to crawl, what it means to move the dead weight of his stiffened body.

"Okay, maybe I can pull you across."

Erik's face is expressionless, clay-like.

"Hang in there, okay? I'm with you, man."

Avery slides away. Another gap of time passes. Erik feels his right arm being jostled. Avery has stripped off his sweater and is tying one arm around Erik's wrist. Erik feels a tug on his arm, a stretching of his body. But it's no good. Something is binding him. The pressure releases on his wrist.

Avery's face slides back into view. "You're frozen in, Erik. I can't move you." His smile is twisted sideways. "You always wanted to be one with the ice, buddy." The smile changes to a deadly serious expression. "Look.

I'm going for the others. With Tom's ladder we'll have you off in a jiff. Margaritas in town tonight. Just hang on, Erik. Hang on until I get back." The smile. The dark eyes. The promise. The fading hope. Then Avery is gone.

Erik can hear scuffling on the ice, then a sloshing of water as Avery moves off. He feels the ice vibrate as Avery gets back onto his skates. He feels a jolt as Avery sprints and lunges across the widening gulf. There comes the faint sound of blades on ice as Avery speeds away toward shore. Erik tries to look up after his friend, but his beard is frozen in place. He closes his eyes in fatigue, but rips them open as his eyelashes begin to freeze. He will not be blind to his fate.

The numbness that invades Erik's body grows into a burning, blistering heat. The heat intensifies as a thin film of water seeps around him. An arctic breeze sweeps down from the hills, nudging the free floating plate further out onto the lake. The evening sun twinkles on the ridge, then fades. The air suddenly chills in a preview of the bitter cold that will come with the night.

Erik wants to look at the world around him, to survey his diminished personal geography. He twists his head, wrenching his frozen beard. He can no longer make the distinction between ice and water, between solid and liquid. Erik wrenches his head again and studies the pale blue sky, hoping the light will keep him alive, the last light of the day.

Later, much later, there are cries from the shore, shouts and calls from his friends. They have come with ropes and picks and life jackets and the aluminum ladder from Tom's car. Changed into dry clothes and warmed with a thermos of hot tea, Avery stands at the edge of the peninsula. He looks across forty feet of open lake to where Erik's inert body lies sprawled on the floating ice, just the way he had left him.

Erik's mind struggles to decipher his friends' calls. He conjures a foggy vision of children playing, gliding on the frozen surface of a canal. He sees his father gently coaxing a small boy in a gray woolen jacket, a red hat, and red mittens to take his first steps on skates, his first steps on the ice. "Come out on the ice, Erik," his father beckons. "Come out onto the ice."

That night, as wisps of steam rise into the harsh, biting air, Erik's plate of ice thickens into a stronger plate into which he is firmly embedded. His bearded cheek is crusted with rime frost, his eyelashes white and frozen together. The drifting plate turns slowly beneath a smear of stars as its passenger seeks other shores. ☆

Chapter 2 | The Living Saint

ARRIET RUPP WAS LED by the flitting of a yellow warbler down a narrow alley between weathered clapboard sheds and carriage houses gray with age. Distracted by the flash of yellow feathers, she nearly bumped into him.

The man wore a rumpled brown suit. He was leaning over to sniff the pale blooms of a lilac. Harriet nudged the gravel with her toe. The man straightened slowly and turned. The bushy mustache all but covered his lips. The dignified brow jutted from a broad forehead. The prominent nose was set between keen, sparkling eyes shaded by arching, inquisitive eyebrows. The long, layered hair was parted and swept back. She recognized him instantly.

He bowed slightly, a look of whimsy softening his creased features. Their eyes met and Harriet felt a charge as his essence poured over her. His kind, otherworldly eyes brought her a sense of reassurance and infused her with a spiritual balm. Here was the man the newspapers dubbed the "Living Saint."

"Hello," she said, feeling awkward for having disturbed his reverie.

He smiled, and color rose to her cheeks. She sidestepped around him. His eyes followed, burning into her with a blend of fascination and amusement. At the end of the block, she turned. He stood dappled by morning sun and shadow, still clutching the lilac bloom, still following her with his eyes. She marveled that she had nearly touched him. His eyes were the last features to imprint on her mind, and she would never forget them. She would never forget that moment, in that alley, in July 1949, in Aspen.

"Charlie, I just had the most remarkable encounter," Harriet reported to her husband after rushing home in a state of excitement. Charlie was sitting in an easy chair by the light of the window in the small living room. He looked up from the book he was reading. "And...?" he said.

"I was walking in the alley and...well, who do you suppose was there?"

Charlie shrugged. "Dr. Albert Schweitzer," she enthused.

"Is that so?"

"Yes. He was just standing there and..." Harriet was suddenly at a loss for words.

"Did he say anything?"

"No. He was just sniffing the lilacs."

"Did you say anything?"

"Well...no. It was just kind of amazing to see him there. He's not as old as I pictured him."

Charlie smiled. "Well, I guess we'll have to wait for tonight to hear what he has to say." Charlie went back to his book.

Harriet suddenly felt silly for sharing her experience. That was for her to hold, so she partitioned a place deep inside her for the knowing eyes and the warm heart.

That night, after a hurried dinner at the Hotel Jerome, Harriet and Charlie joined the festival throng and entered the big white tent in the meadow at the far end of the old horse racing track. There was a mood of excitement, a revival meeting atmosphere that charged the air with great expectations. Harriet looked forward more than ever to hearing Dr. Schweitzer's address, feeling somewhat intimate about him.

Harriet and Charlie sat on a crowded wooden pew under bare lights that dangled from wires strung from poles across the tent. Three heady weeks in Aspen were billed as the Goethe Bicentennial Convocation and Music Festival. It was all inspiring and beautiful and hopeful. Harriet had already listened to the edifying words of Giuseppe Borgese, Jose Ortega y Gasset, and William E. Hocking as they expounded on the finer points of Goethe, his personality, his relationship with Schiller, his travels, his studies of science. Tonight her attention was focused on the man she had caught casually sniffing lilacs in the alley. Now it was Schweitzer's turn to shed light on Goethe, one German to another, one human being to another.

Dr. Schweitzer bowed to five minutes of applause from the grateful audience gathered in the billowing white tent pitched with iron spikes on the mountain meadow. This man, who the world celebrated for his humble virtue, bowed as if he were enduring a cold rain. Harriet thought he looked forlorn and alien amid the tumult of adoration, a sincere man in the throes of unwanted celebrity who only desired to heal the sick, care for the poor, and minister to the dying in remotest Africa. Schweitzer was a small figure at the podium, but a giant persona on the world stage.

Schweitzer's address was billed as an exploration into the life and thought of Goethe on this, Goethe's 200th birthday. The chief organizer of the festival, Walter Paepcke, whom Harriet and Charlie knew peripherally through the University of Chicago, where Charlie was a professor, had introduced the program several days before with his own summary of Goethe: "In his life and in his work," orated Paepcke, "Goethe represented the universality rather than the specialization of knowledge; humanity rather than the nation; the dignity of the individual rather than the power of the state..."

Great accolades, thought Harriet, who mused that Paepcke wielded considerable wealth and power gained by selling mass produced cardboard shipping cartons to the very industries of corporate America which underscored the power of the state. Somehow, it didn't all add up.

Harriet had struggled through some of Goethe's writings in preparation for the Convocation, but found them convoluted and murky. She forced herself to read his famous novel, *The Sorrows of Young Werther*, and thought it sentimental and melodramatic. Even Goethe's *Faust* was not the literary gem it was reputed to be. But then the Convocation wasn't just about Goethe.

Harriet reasoned that this ambitious pageant was more about countering the threat of nuclear war than it was about Goethe, that it was more about promoting world government than it was about the tenets of humanism, that its primary mission was to heal the festering wounds of war that were still raw and painful and had yet to be scabbed over. Some cynics went so far as to claim that Walter Paepcke, because of his

Germanic background, had organized the festival to sanitize the brutal legacy of Germany, which he hoped to restore into the good graces of Western civilization.

Harriet refused to believe that Paepcke and his celebrated collaborators would sponsor the Convocation purely for nationalistic self-interest, or that Dr. Schweitzer would attend if there were any hint of a political agenda. As for Goethe, she felt ill-equipped to judge him, so she accepted the Convocation's assessment that his life was noble and philosophic and enlightened, and that he offered a moral bearing on the uncertainties of the nuclear age, even if that age was two centuries beyond his ken. She was most excited by Schweitzer's presence, and in this she joined an enraptured following who felt the event represented a new height in human striving for universal peace. The presence of the Living Saint lent a spiritual aura to the proceedings and to the nebulous causes behind it.

As the applause slowly faded, Harriet gazed with expectation at Schweitzer who stood in a shaft of light radiating onto the rostrum. Grandiose global transformations aside, she thought that any man who appreciated the sweet scent of lilacs was a good man. She was still unable to identify the essence that had surrounded him in the alley, but it had to do with simple, sincere goodness, a seed that needed planting in many minds. Soon there was not a whisper other than the night breeze that seeped through the flaps of the tent, bearing the cool mountain air. The good doctor cleared his throat, raised his eyes to the audience, and began.

He spoke in French, slowly, methodically, allowing the words to flow in measurable quantities so that those, like Harriet, with limited understanding of French, could grasp a word here and there. Harriet marveled that here stood Schweitzer, a man with German roots, an Alsatian, speaking French to an English language audience, summoning the spirit of Goethe to a tent in the Rocky Mountains of Colorado. The appearance of Schweitzer awakened her to the ambition and reach of the Convocation, which was nothing short of humanistic unity in the wake of a tragic world war that had ended with nuclear bombs. She felt she was part of something extraordinary and historic, and her heart swelled with the meaning of it.

As Schweitzer spoke, Harriet was jarred by the dichotomy of the charitable love this man exuded and the horrors of the Reich that had been vanquished only four years before. She wondered how one man standing tall in a world sullied by war and genocide could project renewed hope for all of humanity. Still, it left her with a nagging question: Could Schweitzer and the dim memory of Goethe overcome the deeds of Hitler, Göring, Goebbels, Hess and all the other monsters? Could small, individual doses of goodness outweigh evil on a grand and ghastly scale?

Dr. Robert Hutchins, at the opening of the Convocation several days before, had suggested as much. "Germany, the bloody battleground," said this handsome, youthful chancellor from Chicago, "must be planted again if the difficulty of the human spirit is to be surmounted..."

Harriet doubted that Goethe or the Living Saint had it within their collective power to replant Germany. She wondered if there could be any satisfactory resolve to the mistakes of the past or whether the scars of history, the wounds of humanity, were better left unhealed as a warning to future generations. Harriet had long ago abandoned her childhood belief that God exerted moral authority over man. How could anyone live through a world war that ended in a nuclear holocaust and still believe in holy intervention?

Every age, she reasoned, needs its saints, living or dead, upon whom it can project virtue. Ever age needs saviors imbued with divine qualities who can elicit hope for the entire race. Every age needs messiahs who sacrifice themselves, or are sacrificed, to become martyrs to the greater good.

Schweitzer's words poured forth in stops and starts through the translator, the urbane Thornton Wilder, who became a medium for Goethe and a channel between Schweitzer and the rapt Aspen audience. Harriet listened intently, trying to assimilate the meanings. Words swirled around her in an esoteric haze. "Purity" and "kindness" lodged in her mind as vital tenets of Schweitzer's message.

"Kindness," translated Wilder as Schweitzer paused to sip water from a glass, "is the supreme manifestation of the spirit of man, a spirit that obliges man to be considerate of others." Wilder paused for dramatic effect. "The man who really finds himself cannot do otherwise than let himself be guided by love, which is the divine element in him."

"Love," repeated Harriet to herself, her lips forming the word. "Love." It was so simple, so obvious, so vague.

Schweitzer then shared a rueful confession, which came through Wilder: "Goethe was human. He possessed within himself the totality of human contradictions. He made mistakes and he lived with them as an imperfect, but striving, man."

Harriet recalled reading about how Goethe had obsequiously served the Grand Duke of Weimar, how Goethe, at the pinnacle of his fame, had cavalierly dismissed Beethoven during a brief and lackluster audience, how Goethe had conjoined in a tempestuous love affair with Marianna, a banker's wife. She realized that Goethe, like all men, had his devils, yet here was a Convocation devoted to his celebrated being.

"Striving," said Wilder, following a passage of French from Schweitzer, "was the key to Goethe's greatness, the representation of his free will. Only by striving could man make a claim for nobility, no matter how futile. In striving lay the potential for the only rational vision of the future, the only path toward hope."

So, mused Harriet, Goethe had concluded that the act of striving, even without success, was ennobling. She had always believed that effort without achievement was an act of futility, that only results warranted the kind of recognition Goethe was now receiving. How strange, she thought, to venerate a man who was revered more, perhaps, for his efforts than for his accomplishments.

At the end, Schweitzer spoke in a near whisper, his gaze elevated above the audience. His final words, which he spoke in English, reverberated through the tent: "We cannot do otherwise than consider Goethe a great, deep, imposing, and, despite all his peculiarities, sympathetic personality."

And then it was over. The tent erupted in thunderous applause as the audience got to its feet. The applause rippled the fabric of the tent with the beating of thousands of hands. There were shouts of praise, hosannas raised to the mountaintops. Tears sparkled in moist eyes. Schweitzer remained at the podium, his head down, his eyes closed.

The faithful flooded from the tent into the cool night beneath a stunning array of stars. Walking home, Charlie reflected that the address was a rapturous moment that could never be equaled in Aspen, or perhaps anywhere in the country, that there are places and times when events transcend the norm. Aspen had become such a place. Harriet said she felt it too, but questioned whether it could last. They walked on in silence, Harriet wondering if the moral force of Schweitzer and the ambiguous ideals of Goethe could influence the world. Would they influence her?

"Does it make you feel different, Charlie, what he said about love being the divine element in man?"

"Well...that's something to ponder."

"I think he's right," she said. "I just hope there's still time."

"You mean time for love to save us from self-annihilation?"

"Yes," said Harriet.

"Do you ever wonder if the human race deserves saving?" suggested Charlie. "It's a valid question, you know."

"But dear, that's what this is all about."

"But isn't it presumptuous that it should start here...in Aspen?"

"Charlie, it has to start somewhere."

Later, when Harriet learned that Schweitzer had been lured to Aspen with a $5,000 donation to fund his leprosy clinic, she was shocked. How parsimonious and manipulative of the organizers to lure him from his mission for such a small gift. How desperate Schweitzer must have been for benefactors that he would leave Africa to speak in a tent halfway around the world, and to be hounded by a celebrity-crazed media on top of it. Harriet thought it must have been humiliating, which she deemed a strange prerequisite for sainthood.

Years later, Harriet understood the allure of Aspen and why the Convocation had been held here. She and Charlie had succumbed to Aspen's spell under Paepcke's coaxing, and, once here, they discovered an uncut gem set amid mountains, valleys and rushing rivers. Aspen was old and decrepit, as were some of the hangers-on who haunted the dusty streets, like ghosts from the last century. Harriet sometimes felt like an interloper, peering at the old-timers in their ramshackle cabins as they, in turn, peered back at her the way bush people stare with misgivings at missionaries.

At Paepcke's suggestion, Charlie had bought a run-down Victorian on Bleeker Street for thirteen hundred dollars. There was no plumbing, just an outhouse near the alley that leaned precariously into the pit below. Charlie had the place fixed up by a local handyman who said his great aunt had lived in that house when the mines were still working. Harriet came to love that small Victorian more than their three-story colonial in Evanston beneath the spreading elms. She and Charlie and their two children spent lovely summers on Bleeker Street. It was here that Charlie was stricken with a first heart attack in 1960, which he dismissed as an aberration of his typically robust health. It was here that a second massive heart attack took Charlie in July of 1963. Harriet found sanctuary in that Victorian because it kept her closest to her memories of Charlie, but also to the warm, soothing spirit she had met in the alley that summer morning, long ago, a spirit that continued to nurture her.

In love with Aspen and the mountains, Harriet and her two children, Ted and Anna, abandoned the Midwest and made Aspen their full-time home. They discovered the joys of winter when on quiet mornings they trudged with wooden skis on their shoulders up the hill to Lift 1. Dapper in pleated woolen slacks and Norwegian sweater, Harriet schussed the snowy slopes and toppled into soft snow that burned against her skin. The children became proficient skiers and, by spring, they all wore deep tans from the Colorado sun.

One blazing sunny day in March, a yodel pealed down from the slope above where Harriet was skiing. She stopped and glanced up Roch Run into a starburst sun gleaming from a deep blue sky. A lone skier rocketed past her making graceful turns. He was one of the famous Austrians, and he swept by her spouting a glimmering rooster tail of snow. As he passed, he touched his cap, yodeled once more, flew over a lip of snow, and disappeared toward the rooftops of the town. Harriet felt a deep romantic attachment to everything Aspen. The place became part of her.

Nights in Aspen were often festive with jazz and cocktails and late nights at the Red Onion or the Golden Horn. The town had a Bohemian air that Harriet found intoxicating. Sometimes she needed help getting home, and some of the men who saw her to her door tried to make love to her, and some of them did. A frivolous atmosphere had overcome the town. It was contagious, and Harriet was susceptible. Her children, now grown, cautioned her gently, then more firmly. One winter night, after a Hotel Jerome jazz party, she fell in a stupor into the soft, deep, comforting snow outside the Victorian. She nearly froze to death before a passerby revived her and brought her to the hospital. Ted and Anna intervened.

Harriet left Aspen to regain her composure in staid old Evanston around staid old friends who did not marvel at skiing or jazz or snow or mountains, as Harriet did. She came to realize that they marveled at very little beyond the confinements of their culture. They ushered her to events at Northwestern, the Art Institute, the Schubert, Ravinia, and Orchestra Hall. They were attentive and observant and stultifying. Harriet loved the arts, but she never forgot the smell of coal smoke, the squeak of snow under leather ski boots, the graceful contours of the mountains, the glow of shimmering golden aspen leaves, the clarity of the mountain air. She never forgot the Living Saint and his illuminating spirit. She romanticized Aspen—her Elysium—during those penitent years in her Midwestern cloister.

Returning to Aspen, years later, in the early '80s, she was shocked by the changes. The town's blithe spirit had been dimmed. The post-war

Bohemians were no longer the vanguards of town spirit. The intellectuals were marginalized by commercial interests and material status. Her son, Ted, had graduated Princeton and came to live with her for a summer before embarking on a career as a stock portfolio manager in New York. Her daughter, Anna, lived with an artist in Sante Fe, then with a poet in San Francisco, then with an architect in Seattle. Harriet's address book was lined with deletions and scrawled phone numbers.

Mired in solitary introspection, the Goethe Convocation became a watershed for Harriet. She viewed her life as either before Goethe or after Goethe, and what came after gradually tore down what had come before. Her children were grown and gone. Charlie was dead. Aspen was forever changed. The memory of Schweitzer was faded and dreamlike. Had she really encountered him in that alley?

Alone in her Victorian, Harriet began her own quest for meaning. She read Thoreau in search of simplicity, but discovered that his path wasn't so simple or so pure. She read Emerson for an understanding of nature, but remained baffled by human nature. She read Socrates and accepted the challenge of knowing herself, but stalled on the enigma of being. She confounded her intellect with random selections from the Great Books, a set of which Charlie had brought to Aspen from Chicago. She attended philosophy lectures, struggled through Mortimer Adler's seminars, basked in beautiful music at the tent, attended ballet, watched art films, and read The New Yorker. She explored her existence as a spelunker probes a cave, albeit with a candle. In the end, she was frustrated by the confession that she knew nothing at all.

She found solace on hikes in the mountains where she trailed Pan through the high temples of rock, timber and snow. The rushing wind and bounding streams sang to her their timeless Druid hymns. She connected with Rousseau and read the poems of Shelley and Wordsworth. She found particular resonance with Wordsworth's "Lines."

To her fair works did Nature link
The human soul that through me ran;
And much it grieved my heart to think
What man has made of man.

Nature became her greatest salve, and she lay in wildflower meadows, her Eden, and listened to the hum of the bees. Renewed by mountain sojourns, she discovered resilience in her aging body. She was reborn daily in the pristine womb of the Creation, an aged child of nature who drew sustenance from the wilds.

A few weeks after her 75th birthday, Harriet fell on the trail coming down from American Lake. She grazed her skull on a rock, fractured her wrist, and broke her hip. She was homebound and bedridden. Inactivity wore her down and there was lasting numbness in her right arm. Her faculties fell away like autumn leaves from wind-scoured trees. Her mind drifted with lassitude between the past and the present, between what was real and what was not.

She had visitors, but forgot them as soon as the door closed behind them. Her ken of awareness narrowed to a minute immediacy. Trapped by age and infirmity in her Aspen Victorian, Harriet gazed from her bedroom window at the skeletal fingers of bare, winter trees. Light snow fell, dancing around her memories. She resigned herself to a peaceful exit, an easy passing. She closed her eyes and let her spirit roam.

Again, she saw the yellow warbler flitting down the alleyway. There she found the Living Saint leaning toward the lilac blooms; the bushy mustache, the creased and smiling face, the bright, sparkling eyes. He spoke to her a single word she could not comprehend, though she struggled for its meaning. Suddenly, her mind cleared and she knew in that moment how deeply he had touched her, how deeply all of it had touched her. He spoke again, whispering to her the one simple, confounding word that encompassed it all: "Love." ☆

Chapter 3 | Moonlight Over Pearl

I T IS A LATE JANUARY AFTERNOON and the ghost town of Ashcroft is drifted-in with snow. The empty frame buildings stand as silent witnesses to a past told in whispers of wind, the hushed purl of the creek, the rattle of a tin roof, the groan of an aged timber. The air is dry and cold, the sun is low.

We ski up the empty, snowpacked road past stark aspens whose long slanting shadows stripe the snowpack with geometric patterns. In my backpack I carry a Nalgene bottle wrapped in a string of Tibetan prayer flags. I've never carried cargo like this before, and I have packed it carefully, cautious not to bruise the contents, even though it can never be bruised again.

Brent leads off with a strong stride, followed by Jason and Todd. I watch them go, taking time to adjust my poles, lengthening them for the uphill, twisting the shafts tight, snugging my gloves into the straps. I set off with an easy pace on the long, gradual hill toward Pine Creek.

Beyond the Cookhouse, we spread out to cross the big slide path, the one that killed a lone woman skier years before, burying her until June. We follow the faint ski track off the main road, past the last electric pole, beneath the last telephone line, beyond the last stretch of pavement buried deep under the snow. We regroup in the first big meadow for the traditional taste of single malt.

"To Mark!" toasts Jason, holding the flask aloft, touching each of us with his bright blue eyes. He passes the flask and we each take a fiery gulp, a ritual that Mark instigated for his love of Islay spirits. He's not here to drink with us, so we toast him appropriately.

We set off again, spreading out by habit and desire, each of us seeking the vacuum of a profound silence that emanates from the mountains. All I can hear is the faint rasp of my skis against snow, the jab of my ski poles, the rhythm of my breathing. To measure each moment by these simple components provides the deeply meditative beauty of ski touring. Place it in a sublime mountain setting and the feeling becomes euphoric.

Soon, the sun twinkles and dips below the ridge, plunging us into shade. A wave of dense, frigid air flows down the valley and washes over us, dropping the temperature by ten degrees. My face burns with the cold, intensifying the bite of the air in my nose and throat, and I can feel the flesh of my cheeks grow stiff and leathery. Our exhales billow into fleeting vapor trails as late sun transforms lofty pinnacles and spires into fluted candelabras. A jagged peak glows pink where a snow plume rises in a pastel brush stroke painted by the jet stream. To the east, Venus, the bright glinting planet, sparkles in a deepening purple field, marking the advance of the darkness we have come for.

Climbing into the narrow valley of upper Castle Creek, we leave longer gaps between us to cross the big avalanche runs. Space leaves each of us in a pleasurable solitude, entranced by our own rhythms and thoughts. At one point we ski above the rush of Castle Creek where it has worn a gorge into the granite, its timeless cascades muffled by snow. We pass through groves of bare aspens and beneath dark arches of thick-limbed spruce and fir. The walls of the valley narrow as the peaks rise higher. In the last faint light of dusk we arrive at a small, picturesque, stone cabin tucked into the timber at the edge of a deep ravine. Snow is thick on the rooftop, drooping from the eaves in soft, overhanging folds.

We glide down to the cabin where a shard of yellow lamplight streaks from a window and illuminates a patch of snow. The sharp smell of smoke is in the air. We take off our skis and lean them against a huge stack of split firewood. The entry is bunker-like and dark, and we clump noisily down a walkway beneath a low shed roof. The latch is lifted and the heavy, iron-banded door is opened. We enter what feels like a medieval cloister.

Maggie stands by the open door and welcomes us into the light, the warmth. We sniff the fragrance of spices from her kitchen. She lives here alone since her husband drowned while kayaking a wild river, a man we all knew and respected. A strong woman, still young and pretty, with thick red hair and quick, green eyes, she abides in this mountain monastery in penitent solitude. The hut has become her refuge, her place of mourning. She greets us with firm handshakes and a fleeting smile. She knows why we've come. I hand her two bottles of wine pulled from my pack. She nods, indicates the table, and disappears into the small kitchen.

We strip off coats, hats and gloves and hang them on wrought iron hooks. We take places at the table where she fills our wine glasses with inky cabernet. She goes to the kitchen and returns with steaming bowls of spicy vegetable soup, which she carries on a big tray. She places a pan of thick cornbread and a dish with a big slab of butter in the middle of the table.

"Where's your place?" I ask, taking a seat.

"This is for you."

"No, Maggie, we'd like you to join us. Please"

She shakes her head then quickly surveys the table. Seeing that everything in its place, she smiles and returns to the kitchen. We look at each other over the steaming soup, the dark wine, wondering if words should be said. No one speaks. Jason raises his glass for a silent toast. We raise our glasses and drink, then spoon up the delicious soup.

We eat silently and take in this austere habitation. Kerosene lanterns bathe the stone walls with dim, yellow light. Vintage snowshoes and wooden skis hang on the walls among photographs of men in military uniforms and mountains festooned with glaciers. The heat stove, a huge block of cast iron as large as a washing machine, consumes logs cut and split from seasoned avalanche debris. I work my toes in my thick woolen socks on the smooth plank floor, feeling the cold seep up.

"There's plenty more," says Maggie. We refill our soup bowls with a ladle from the large pot she holds before each of us. It would be rude to refuse seconds. After we're done, she officiously clears our plates, then empties the last wine bottle into our glasses. The blood red of the cabernet catches the candlelight, glowing deep ruby red. When the dishes are cleared, Maggie pulls up a stool and joins us for honey-sweetened ginger tea and chocolate chip cookies she's baked herself.

"I'm glad you stopped by," she says. "I might lose my social skills if I'm left alone here too long...not that I had any in the first place."

"You don't have to worry about that with us," I reassure her. "We appreciate the hospitality."

"That's why this cabin is here."

We knew the man who built the cabin, who lost his son, Maggie's husband, to the river. He never bore any malice, knowing the risks very well himself. The old man came from Austria, emigrating after the war. He hand-built this cabin from stone, by himself, and in doing so, he became like the mountains—hard, strong, enduring. He showed his strength in the accepting manner in which he outlived his son. Life and death were interchangeable to him, two equal sides of being human. When the old man passed, they buried him beneath the rocks and soils of these mountains in a simple and beautiful pine box he hand-crafted himself, for that purpose, measured to his exact dimensions, fitted to his own body.

The fire pops in the stove, filling gaps in our lagging conversation. Through the front window comes a faint glow. The moon is on the rise. She notices and busies herself clearing plates, cups and saucers. We push away from the table and begin lacing our leather boots, sitting on hand hewed wooden benches before the stove. This is the last warmth we'll have until we cross the pass and reach the hut on the other side, so we absorb it greedily.

She motions me aside. "How will you do it?" she asks quietly, discreetly.

"Do what?"

"The ashes."

"At the pass. That's what Mark wanted."

"Which side of the pass?"

"Hmmm. I hadn't thought about that."

"He was your brother. You should know."

"I guess we'll figure that out when we get there."

She stares hard at me. "It should be your decision...yours alone. When I had Mike's ashes, they tried to tell me what to do, even the old man did, but I wouldn't listen. Mike was my husband! I took them and did what I wanted. Do you know where I put them? I poured them in the creek when no one else was there. That was between me and Mike. The old man understood when I told him, and then he cried. I'd never seen him cry before. No one had."

"That took guts."

"It was my will against the family, that's all."

"Knowing that family, that's saying a lot."

She nods and glances at my pack. "Can I see him? Can I hold him?"

My eyebrows arch in surprise. "You want to look at...?"

"Please, I need to. Is that okay?"

I rustle through my pack and hand her the Nalgene bottle, wrapped in prayer flags. She takes the bottle in her hands and stares at it. She fingers a prayer flag and a subtle change flashes across her features. She emits a high wail, shoves the bottle at me, and darts into the kitchen.

Jason approaches. He is dressed and ready. "What happened?" he whispers, nodding toward the kitchen. "She wanted to see the bottle," I shrug, carefully replacing the Nalgene in my pack.

Jason raises his eyebrows. "Why?"

I shake my head. "I've gotta settle up with her. Go on, if you want. I'll be right behind." Jason nods and takes his gloves and hat off the hooks above the stove. Todd and Brent follow suit.

Maggie reappears with a paper sack. Tears streak her face. "Here're some more cookies. Take them, please," she says, blinking.

"Thanks. Thanks for everything. It was really a good dinner. Tell me what we owe. I'd like to pay up before we go."

"You don't owe me a thing."

"Oh, yes we do."

"Catch up with me later. But just remember, when you're up there..." she grips my arm, "...this is for you, not for him. He knew what you would need. That's why he wanted it like this."

"Hey, thanks."

The others say good night and file out past the thick, heavy door. She stands mute as they stomp down the walkway toward the snow. She locks her eyes with mine with a look that speaks more than any words, a look of great need and vulnerability. "Wouldn't it be better if you stayed here, with me? We could take care of him, just the two of us, like family."

"No way, Maggie, these guys were his best friends."

"Your brother and I..." she blinks back tears. "Mark was very special to me. Maybe you didn't know, but he came here, after he learned he was sick." She bites her lip. "Stay with me tonight. I'd need to tell you about it."

"Maggie... No, I can't."

"Sometime, then, so we can talk about Mark. There are things you should know about him...and me. There are things you should know about his divorce from Sadie, about what happened between them."

"Maybe I don't need to know."

"But you should know."

"Why are you telling me this?"

"You should know everything. I don't want to be the only one holding it. Do you understand what that's like for me?"

"No, Maggie, I don't."

"Look. If my skis are here, I'm here. You're always welcome. I hope you'll come. We have a lot to talk about." She releases my arm and steps back, her eyes bright, glistening, unwavering.

"Yeah, well...thanks again." I sling on my pack and step into the darkened entryway. She remains by the door. I can feel her eyes on me. The murky interior of the hut is empty now except for the memories framed on the thick stone walls.

"Be safe," she says, then pulls the big door shut, sealing it like a vault that safeguards her sorrows. I take a deep breath of the burning cold air. A sense of urgency hastens my steps down the entryway and out under the starlit sky.

"What was that about?" asks Jason.

"Fuck if I know."

The warmth in my belly, glowing radiantly, takes the sting out of the frosty night. I quickly stretch on climbing skins, snap into my bindings, snug up pole straps, and join the others on the trail at the edge of the clearing. A glance back at the cabin reveals a tiny sliver of yellow light seeping from the window. Maggie is watching us, her silhouette dark against the lantern light. She's given us food and warmth, but left me with a haze of unanswered questions about Mark.

We stick together on the steep trail, passing through stands of black timber where stars glimmer in the openings overhead. Our headlamps light the way with wavering beams. We cross a narrow bridge where the creek murmurs beneath a thick mantle of snow. We emerge above tree-line into the open basin where there is only rock and snow. We stop to regroup before cutting the long traverse toward the pass.

"She must get mighty lonely in that place," I say, trying to come to terms with what just happened.

"Maybe you'd like to keep her warm some night," chides Todd.

"Careful, dude," warns Jason. "The old man's ghost watches over that cabin. Weird things can happen there."

"Ghosts don't bother me."

"You're more afraid of women," suggests Brent.

"Yeah, women..."

I don't divulge what Maggie said. That's something for me to work over. All I can figure is that loss and loneliness make strange bedfellows of some people, my brother included. I can't quite see how Mark fit into Maggie's life, but these things seem to happen. Maggie is just one more source of amazement, a personal revelation. Secrets don't die with those who hold them closest. They live on among an ever expanding group of sharers, the trustees of confidence who parcel out shares with each indiscreet disclosure. Mountain towns have no secrets.

Brent sets off on a contour across the basin. We follow him toward the promise of moonlight, now a bright glow on the high ridges above us. Our exhales form passing clouds in our headlamp beams as we follow Brent's meandering route through gnarled and twisted trees. Wind gusts stir the icy air. Our skis creak and grate against hard, wind-slabbed snow that barely yields to a ski edge.

Above tree-line we cross the wavering boundary of shadow and light. Suddenly, we're bathed in a silvery sheen. The rising moon, round and full, creeps above the notch of Pearl Pass, floating in a stellar vastness and washing out the stars. The craters and mountains of the moon are distinct to our naked eyes. Around us the shapes of mountain peaks produce a moonscape of their own. The snowy basin glows as with phosphorescence. Ice crystals glint back the moonlight with infinite facets, mirroring the faint sparkles of stars millions of light years away.

The air is thin and biting cold at 12,000 feet. The atmosphere seems nonexistent. The heavens expand overhead with surreal clarity. A gust of wind sweeps out of nowhere, launching a spindrift of snow that whirls, encircles us, and moves across the undulating basin with a seething sweep of ice-filled air. We stop on the rocky knoll just below the pass, from where we'll make the final ascent. This is the last potential avalanche slope, so we'll take it one at a time. We pack away our headlamps, our eyes fully adjusted to the moonlight. We stand quietly, listening.

Out of the silence, booming like a thunderclap, then growing into a pervasive roar, a jet streaks across the night sky. The silvery missile rips through the blackness, leaving a glittering wake. The noise fades to a distant rumble, then disappears, making the silence even more intense. I wonder about the people in that airplane, picturing them in their plastic seats, breathing recycled air, rushing somewhere at tremendous speed. How totally isolated are we from them, travelers in different worlds.

"This is fuckin' awesome!" says Jason, breaking the silence.

"He knew it would be like this," agrees Todd.

"He probably knows it still," says Brent.

"If he does, he's a happy spirit," I suggest.

"It's just how he wanted it," says Todd. "A perfect night."

Brent goes first, tracking up the final pitch to the crest of the ridge. Then goes Jason, followed by Todd. I watch the silhouettes of my friends against the stars, the moon, the snow. Standing on that knoll, gazing up into the night sky, there is nothing between me and all of time and space, all that has ever been and ever will be. Here is eternity, seen in one mind-numbing glance. My soul fills with the enormity of it, the speck of my being humbled by what surrounds me.

I push hard to join the others. My lungs burn, my heart throbs. Cresting the ridge, I take in the panorama of high mountains stretching in all directions. Star Peak stands to the east, lording over the night sky with stunning symmetry. Beyond Star Peak, the Sawatch Range stretches to the south in big, hummocky, snowcapped summits. Peaks encircle us to the far edge of every horizon. We stand quietly, humbly, happily marooned in an infinite vastness. The wind wisps around us, bitter and cold.

"Well, what are we waitin' for?" says Brent, stomping his skis on the wind-hardened snow.

I drop my pack, pull off a glove, and dig through my gear. My hand locates the Nalgene bottle. I pull it out and shake it gently. I hold the bottle and realize I don't even feel the weight of him, burned to ash by white hot fire, the gravelly remnants dry and rattling in the water bottle he carried everywhere. I'm holding what's left of his once strong body, a warm, pulsing body that decayed in a matter of months into a skeletal framework out from which he intensely gazed during the final hours of his life. I watched him weather like the rotting of wood, the rusting of iron, the melting of ice.

"Words, anybody?" I mumble, my face stiff with the cold. There is only a shuffle of skis, the groan of a ski pole tip prying against the hard snow.

"What are we supposed to say?" asks Todd

"Hell, I don't know," says Jason. 'Adios, mo-fo'?"

"Oh, that's a touching send-off."

"Dude," says Brent. "You know that if it was you or me in that bottle, that's what he would've said. Mark wasn't exactly the most reverent guy."

"He and I used to talk about death," I explain. "That was when we were in the fastest pulse of life. Death was this incredible contrast. We felt so far removed from it. He used to say that life and death were like the half moon. The bright side shines silver against the faint outline of the dark side. We were always in the light, looking at the dark, wondering about it."

The wind wells up, hits us with a gust, then dies away in a soft sigh. The moon shines down from the blackness, too bright to look at without squinting.

"What about his kids, his boys?" asks Brent. "Did he make you promise like he made me?"

"Oh, yeah. He thought all that through," laughs Jason. "He made me a fucking list!"

"The last time I saw him he could hardly talk," says Todd, "but he made it very clear that we have a lot of places to take those kids, places he wanted to take them himself."

"I told him we'd divvy it up," I say, "that we would each choose a place. He made me swear to it, like a covenant, and that seemed to give him some peace."

"I told him I'd show them around the South San Juans," says Jason, "the place where the last grizzly was killed."

"I said I'd take them out to Slickhorn," says Todd, "to the Perfect Kiva. Man, he loved that place."

"Pyramid," says Brent. "I pledged to take them up Pyramid. Mark and I climbed Pyramid when we first moved here…in a snowstorm."

"That leaves the Gila for me," I conclude, "the fly-bitten, snake-infested Gila—home of the javelinas—one of the wildest places we ever knew."

"The Esplanade," intones Brent. "Who's going to take them there?

Who's going to show it to them the way he saw it? Anybody up for the death march from Matkat to Supai?"

"What about the Winds?" asks Jason. "He loved that place, too."

"I'm surprised he didn't want himself scattered over all those places," says Todd. "A thimbleful for every mountaintop, every canyon, every nook and cranny."

"That would take a lifetime," I say.

"He didn't want himself spread too thin," surmises Brent.

"Pearl," I conclude. "Pearl by moonlight; that's what he said. That's what he wanted. Right here and now."

Brent shuffles his skis. "Well, can you imagine anything better?"

We scan the basin, stare up at the stars, allow our souls communion with everything we see and feel. We're caught up in a mood of reverence and awe. The time has come.

"Okay, then." I jiggle the Nalgene bottle.

"Hold it," says Jason. "Isn't there's something more? Something more we should say?"

Nobody speaks. I hold the Nalgene bottle against my chest and invite the feelings to flow. There are no words that come with them. Slowly, I unscrew the lid. I take a deep breath and feel the cold burn down my throat and into my lungs. I look up at the stars. The bright smear of the Milky Way is directly overhead.

"Mark didn't want this to be all mopey, for God's sake," says Jason. "Shit, it feels like a fucking funeral."

"It is a fucking funeral!" answers Todd.

"Not his kind of funeral," argues Jason. "Somebody say something funny, something that would make him laugh the way he always made us laugh. That's what he'd want."

Silence. My ears are ringing. I can feel the beating of my heart.

"Oh, just do it!" urges Todd.

I step forward and hold out the Nalgene bottle. "Good-bye, my brother."

I swing my arm fast, in a big arc, flinging the contents high into the cold night air. The moonlight catches the dust in a silvery shimmer that floats momentarily. Suddenly, a gust of wind rises from the basin, catches the cloud of dust, and flings it back. A hail of dust and grit stings our faces and speckles our jackets. Some of it gets into my mouth. I blink to clear my eyes.

"Aw, shit!" Brent sputters, brushing off his face.

"Damnit, anyway!" exclaims Todd, dusting the fine, white powder off his parka.

Jason had ducked his head to avoid the fall-out. Now he raises his face to the moon, laughing. He raises his arms and hoots. Brent lets out a whoop. We laugh until the tears are freezing on our cheeks, until our stomachs hurt, until everything is let go.

"Nice of Mark to make one last appearance," says Jason. "His timing was impeccable."

We strip off our climbing skins and stow them in our packs, then sideslip over the pass, metal edges rasping against corrugations of sastrugi. We traverse the moonlit basin toward Star Peak, angling down to the black timber, to the anticipated warmth of the hut.

Near the trees, the smell of wood smoke wafts around us. Our friends from Crested Butte are there, deep within the shadows of old growth spruce and fir where smoke wisps from the stovepipe. The others ski into the darkness. I pause for a last look at the moon. It has reached its zenith, mimicking the arc of the summer sun. Its silvery rays seem to be passing right through me.

I catch up to the others at the hut, a log-built refuge among old growth spruce. We step out of our bindings, clamber across the porch, push open the wooden door. There is a welcome rush of warm, moist air. A fire glows in the stove. A dim light comes from a candle lantern. Our friends are in their bunks.

"How'd it go on the pass?" one of them whispers from his sleeping bag.

"It was perfect," I reply, "just perfect."

We settle into our bunks, our feet deep in our down bags. Soon, the slow, steady breathing of slumbering chums competes with the hissing, spitting water caldron on top of the cast iron stove where lumps of snow melt for tomorrow's coffee. From my bunk in the loft, seen through a small, frost-rimmed window, Star Peak shines brightly. I crank open the window and sniff the cold air. A breeze sighs through the trees.

That night, in a waking moment, I feel an irritation; there's something digging into my side. I work my hand into my bag and feel something under my shirt. What turns up in my fingers is a grainy nugget, a pea-sized piece of bone that somehow got down my collar. I set it carefully on the window sill and smile, wondering about Mark, about the choices he made and those over which he had no control. It's often the latter, the unintended, that dictate the direction of our lives.

Sleep comes fitfully, and I observe the moon's progress through the tiny window at the head of my bunk. Shadows stretch and reconfigure as the moon swings west. By early morning, moonglow is no match for the fierce fireball of the rising sun. The two orbs exchange prominence until dawn washes out the moon's dreamscape, banishing the ethereal until the next moonrise. ☆

Chapter 4 | The Piano Teacher

AS LU YANG ENTERS the white, billowing music tent a soft undercurrent of recognition runs through the audience. To the old teacher's ears it sounds like a wave washing over a pebbled beach, a wave that engulfs Yang as he seats himself in the front row, cordoned off by a ribbon that marks his privilege.

The audience gathers in the rows behind him to witness the performance of his prize pupil, whom Yang can still picture as a wisp of a girl who had entered his studio seven years before, at nine years old. Soon, the rapt gaze and nervous attention of the audience will hold her as the grown woman she has become. Yang remembers how that same intensity had held him many years before when, as only a boy, he had performed his first major piano concerto. With that memory comes the sharp, familiar stab of failure.

Moments before, in the dressing room, he had tried to calm her, but there was no quelling her exultant mood. She beamed at him with the bright promise of youth, her eyes glinting with deep inner strength and limitless courage. He gave her hands a warm clasp, trying to infuse them with the power of his belief in her. "Focus," he admonished, and she smiled and nodded knowingly.

From his front row seat in the music tent, Yang gazes at the piano, elevated on stage like a casket ready for visitation, the lid gaping open. He recalls the day when his career as a teacher had begun at the same moment that his life as a performer had ended. One had begot the other, as if that had been the intent.

Yang will soon judge his student, just as Yang's teacher had judged him in the recital hall in New York so long ago. The Czech master was morose during Yang's debut because the rigidity in Yang's fingers revealed his greatest failing—timidity. There was no fire, no spark, and that was unpardonable for a performance musician. Yang recalls how he had stood from the piano to tepid applause, perspiration running down his body. Mediocrity was more crushing than death. He would never perform again.

The life of a teacher has been good to Yang. His crisis of identity receded over time and he felt a surge of pride from his students as they reached greatness. During the forty years of his tutelage, many of his finest students joined faculties at some of the best conservatories in the world. Three former students had become composers; one was conducting a prominent chamber orchestra.

But it was the Romanian girl, Eva Fontescue, who challenged Yang the most with her tempers and mercurial moods. It is her debut today that weighs upon him with the utmost gravity. Her success will be his success, and he realizes that if he is ever going to produce a great concert pianist, it will be Eva. She alone can salvage his standing, his pride.

The audience settles into their seats and rustles their programs. The lights dim. The audience garble dies away. He worries suddenly that he has not given Eva enough or that he simply does not have enough to give. Either way, it is too late now.

Eva strides onto the stage with a graceful, dance-like gait, swinging a luster of long, shining brown hair, her tall, thin body wrapped in a mauve satin dress. She smiles to the appreciative audience, and it is a smile that arcs over Yang's head like a rainbow. She bows deeply to the left and again to the right, then to the middle where her eyes lock for a moment with Yang's. Like a soldier, she stands straight up and marches resolutely to the piano. She sits at the bench and measures the distance to the keyboard with her arms and fingers.

Yang takes a deep breath and feels his heart race. His wizened face tenses into a pained grimace that mocks her easy smile. She strikes the first chord, and soon her fingers are weaving up and down the keyboard. Her body sways like a reed in a stream. The piano jumps to life as if it has been plugged in. The tent suddenly fills with sound.

Complex passages are connected seamlessly by a rush of spirit and joy. Eva's focus is complete. There is nothing between her and the music but the long, facile fingers and the heart and mind that commands them. He witnesses her mastery as never before, knowing that she is in the throes of something grand and elegant and beyond herself.

Yang feels his rigidity soften. His fear abates because he knows that Eva possesses herself fully. Or perhaps it is the music that possesses them all. Yang no longer feels Eva's presence, or even his own. It is only the music that exists, and it comes from a depth of feeling that is tapped from the ages, something innate and visceral and human.

Eva has leaped a barrier that Yang, in his brief performance career, could never surmount. She brings to the stage a blend of pathos and wonder, vivacity and elegance, technique and sensuality. Yang feels her power in the lifting of his heart, the flight of his soul. Eva pauses at the break between movements. She looks as if she, too, is amazed by her agile interpretation. Then she plunges into the most difficult movement. Articulating each note without hesitation, she sweeps into and through it with the raw instinct of genius.

Yang is suddenly overwhelmed by the force of Eva's playing, as if witnessing something primordial and wild. He is scorched by Eva's passion and he sees in her a woman, mature and ennobled. She is now the master and he the student. What she teaches him is total abandonment to the expression of music and to the tempo and rhythm of life. The music is transcendent and devastating. It crushes something deep inside him.

The key change for the last measures catches him by surprise, as if he has never heard it before. He is jolted when she hits the final chords. Suddenly, she is standing at the reverberating piano, the atmosphere electrified. She faces the audience, naked to their prying eyes and snap judgments. Her being is infused with a harmonic resonance that fills the tent with the echo of the last chord.

The audience is suddenly on their feet, a rush of pleasure and pride swelling with their cheers and shouts and applause. The sound is like a downpour on a tin roof. Yang stands slowly, unsteadily, his mouth open, gaping at Eva. How has she learned to perform like this, to transpose such beauty from notes printed on a page? Surely it has not come from him. Her success is hers, alone.

He recognizes in Eva what he has never seen in himself, a free, exultant spirit. Has Yang ever really understood the expressive force of music, or is his musicality merely technical? The old teacher watches Eva with new eyes as she bows left and right while the house thunders. When she looks down upon him, his heart palpitates. When she bows slowly to him—only to him—his composure withers and he lowers his head in deep humility.

"That's her teacher," someone whispers. Faces turn, and the applause engulfs him. Tears flood his downcast eyes. ☆

Chapter 5 | Chalmer's Paradise

T HE THUD OF HORSE HOOVES announces their approach. A cloud of red dust rises from a sage-covered flat, diffusing the low rays of the morning sun. Chalmer's, a compact, grizzled old man, rides a big black mule. Tom, much younger, light brown hair and a sandy beard, follows on a chestnut mare, a packhorse in tow. The air is pungent with sage. Chalmers sings lustily. His voice sounds as if there's gravel in his throat.

> "...with a hat on her head
> and a man in her bed
> she awoke with a start one day-ee
>
> and she said with a sigh
> 'til the day that I die
> Ohio's the place I will stay-ee..."

Tom keeps time by tapping his fingers on the saddle horn. He chuckles over Chalmers' song, the rough, booming voice, and a whoop at the end of each verse. Following Chalmers on his mule provides Tom a rare concert through the unfolding, limitless country. They are well stocked with venison stripped from a doe Tom shot three days before. The morning sun bears down, tempered by a cool breeze from the west. The saddle partners move through a rugged landscape of canyons, rivers and mountains that define their 19th century Eden.

It is mid-day when they follow a dry arroyo down into a wide river valley dotted with stands of tall cottonwoods where a glinting, meandering river flows in no particular hurry. White blooms dangle on the chokecherries and cotton balls dot the serviceberries. The air is fragrant with the tangle of life along the river and there are plentiful signs of elk and deer. Chalmers turns his mule upstream and they follow the river where trout laze in limpid pools. Occasional rapids fill the air with the rush of whitewater. The sound of the water bids them welcome.

"Hold up there, Chalmers. How about we try a little fishin'?"

The old man is happy to sit for a while and fill his pipe in the shade of a tree. Tom cuts a willow, ties on a section of line, and baits the hook with a bluebottle fly he catches with a sweep of his hand through a swarm around the horses. Tom fits a split shot piece of lead onto the line and crimps it into place with his teeth. In two casts, Tom has a fat trout with bright red sides squirming on the hook and bending the willow nearly double. In half an hour, he has landed four fat fish. Chalmers has stoked a fire with cottonwood deadfall.

"You know, Chalmers," Tom says later, leaning against the tree, his stomach full, "I'm gettin' mighty fond of this here life."

"Sure, sure, son. There's a flow to it, just like that river." Chalmers puffs his pipe, his bushy white beard curling around the pipe stem, his narrow-slit eyes peering at the water. "Just follow the stars and the sun and the moon and the wind. Why, it's the way man was meant to live, not in houses with fences and ill-fittin' clothes. That's where man went wrong, thinkin' he needed to keep to one place." Another thoughtful puff and a cloud of tangy tobacco smoke fills the air. "Nope, a man needs to keep movin'. He needs to see the country and feel it in his bones. That's the true nature of man."

"Who put all them notions in your head?" asks Tom.

"Why, I did," answers the old man. "It's called contemplation."

Tom shakes his head. He's feeling scrappy and he knows how to get a rise out of the old mountain man. "Contemplation got nothin' to do with fishin' or skinnin' a deer or tryin' to stay alive in the wilds. Contemplation got nothin' to do with livin', so why waste your time on it?"

The old man taps out his pipe. "Look'a here, son. When you study your own life—and it's something you ought to do because only man, out of all the animals, can do it—you begin to understand what it means to live a good life. Any man that don't take the time to contemplate life and his place in it aint no better than any old cow in the herd."

"I known plenty 'o men who warn't no smarter'n cows," asserts Tom, "and a lot of 'em do just fine. Maybe animals is all we was meant to be, Chalmers."

"That's where you're wrong," exclaims the old man. "Man is man. We're separate from the rest of the animals on account of our ability to reason, to think, to reflect. Listen here, son. Because we got the ability to reason—and contemplate things—we can make intelligent decisions on how we treat other people and the world around us. What makes those decisions sound are the values we hold."

"Well, what the hell good do values do a man when his life depends on his eyes, his ears and his strength? Bein' a good animal is all most men need."

"Blame it!" says Chalmers, his face reddening. "That's just the trouble. Most men are satisfied with the animal in 'em. What they're missing are the values that make us human."

"Seems to me," chuckles Tom, "values is what gets men fightin,' cause nobody can agree on 'em."

"Sure, you got a point there, son, but there are certain values all men agree on, like freedom, the kind of freedom you and me got right here, the kind of freedom that river has by flowin' on and on and on."

"Well," reflects Tom, smug with a stomach full of fish, "I aint interested in no values. I'm interested in livin' the best life the good Lord can provide me. I'm interested in takin' what's mine."

"Then you're nothin' but a brute animal," barks Chalmers, taking up a stick and prodding a cloud of ashes from the fire. He sits up straight and points his pipe stem at Tom. "If you did more thinkin' than doin', you'd be more of a man."

"But I'm already a man," quips Tom, straightening his angular shoulders, "or aint that plain to yuh?"

"That aint enough! You gotta have the wisdom to know that you're part of somethin' bigger...that you're part of mankind."

"Mankind, huh? I known plenty 'a men who aint very kind."

Chalmers shakes his head. "You're not getting' what I'm getting' at." He scratches his head with his pipe stem, probing his thick thatch of gray hair. "Look, you ever hear of what they call phi-lo-so-phy?"

Tom shakes his head. "Nope."

"Ah! I thought so. Well, let me tell you, Tom, there were men two thousand years ago in a place called Greece who invented philosophy. That was back when people was first figuring out they had minds to think with. These philosophers, they started in at the very beginnin', tryin' to describe everything that makes a man tick, everything that makes the world turn."

"Was you around then, Chalmers?"

The old man glares at Tom, turns away, and mumbles his frustration.

Tom picks up a rock and tosses it into the river with a splash. He watches the ripples drift with the current. "Well, why'd they do all that figurin' for?"

Chalmers studies the ever changing hues and shades of the flowing water. "Because they wanted to know what happiness is, that's what for."

"Hell, Chalmers," says Tom, playfully. "I know what happiness is. It's feelin' good, like I feel right now." He clasps his hands behind his head, leans back against the cottonwood, and smiles up at the sky with satisfaction.

"Then you're a damned fool!" grumbles Chalmers, his hackles raised.

"I may be a damned fool," says Tom, still smiling, "But I'm a happy fool, and I aim to stay that way for as long as the good Lord will allow."

Chalmers puffs the dead embers in his pipe, then spits out a residue of tar. "You must think a lot of this Lord of yours, but I'll wager you don't know nothin' about him."

"Don't need to...not so long as he keeps me happy," grins Tom, feeling a perverse pleasure in getting under the old man's hide. "Anyhow, can a fella be any happier than I am right now?"

Chalmers growls low. "Happiness is more than a gutful 'a fish. Them

Greek philosophers figured there was degrees of happiness and that the highest happiness is when a man seeks wisdom. That's what bein' a philosopher is all about." Chalmers clamps the empty pipe into his mouth and folds his arms across his chest with a resolute nod.

"You mean...they decided that happiness was being like they was," goads Tom. "Sounds to me like they was pattin' themselves on the back. Answer me this," says Tom with a mischievous glint in his eye. "If them philosophers was so happy, why'd they go around worryin' about happiness all the time? Why couldn't they just be happy and let it go at that?"

Chalmers slowly removes his pipe from his teeth. He speaks with quiet force. "Because they couldn't stop thinkin' about the meanings of everything. They was driven to work out the mysteries of their existence, to square themselves against all creation, and they dedicated their lives to it."

"Well," laughed Tom, "that aint my idea of happiness."

"That's because you're no philosopher you...you...stubborn son of a mule!"

"Whoa...whoa!" says Tom. "This philosophizin' sure aint makin' you very happy. Say, where'd you get all this stuff, anyway, Chalmers? Why can't you just settle for the here and now, like I do?"

The old man is quiet for a moment as he looks across the river at the willows swaying in the breeze. "That was another life," he muses. "Guess I learned just enough to get me into trouble by askin' too many blame questions. That's what got Socrates killed, you know; askin' too many questions."

"They killed this fella...Sockerteez, you say...just for askin' questions?" returns Tom.

"Socrates! His name was Socrates."

"Well, what kind of country was they livin' in where you couldn't ask no questions?"

"Place called Athens...big Greek city. The leaders of Athens...they didn't like Socrates because he made 'em nervous askin' about things like justice and ethics and fairness."

"Askin' questions oughtn't to be no crime."

"Well...Socrates was a teacher, and he went on teachin' children how to ask them same questions, and that's what really riled 'em up."

"So?"

"So, they put him on trial and sentenced him to death. Socrates drank some poison and killed hisself."

"Killed hisself? That don't sound so smart. Why'd he do that?"

"Because it was right and proper, and it was the law," retorts Chalmers. "Socrates done the right thing."

"Killin' hisself was the right thing? I don't get it."

"That's because you're too damned young and ignorant to understand philosophy."

Tom pulls his knife from a leather sheath and begins whittling on a stick. He glances at Chalmers. "So how'd you pick it up, then?"

"Books," says Chalmers, as if uttering a foreign word. "Hell, son, I was headed to the university, but I never did go."

"Well, why the hell not?"

"The war come along. I joined up. After that I pushed west and...well, here I am. I aint never gone back, but that philosophy stuck with me, and I been contemplatin' on it ever since."

"What'd you come out here for?"

"I dunno. Lookin' for somethin', I guess. Hell, I'm still lookin'."

"I come lookin' for somethin', too" says Tom. "Thought I might find me a pot 'a gold, a nice place of my own, maybe even the right woman. Hell, I thought I might find me all three at once. Now, I don't know. Maybe I found what I set out to find and it's right here on this river, right here by this fishin' hole. Maybe this is as far as I need to go. But there's still something inside me wants a place I can call my own...a piece of land."

Chalmers turns and studies Tom. "Plenty of young fools think they want to settle, build a place, own a few head of horses, maybe some cattle. Pretty soon they got themselves a ranch to look after. Then they's needin' a wife to cook for 'em. Then she's wantin' children to look after. Pretty soon the two of 'em grow old wonderin' what ever happened to their precious time on earth."

Tom stretches his legs. "Aw, I'm just tryin' out some ideas, contemplatin', you might say. Hell, I got my whole life ahead of me, and who's to say I couldn't raise a family and still have time to clear out on my own when I'm your age? You yourself said you had a wife once."

"Yeah, I did, but God saw clearer'n I did, and He took her, leavin' me to my natural ways. No, Tom, I seen it happen to my first partner, fella named Abner Sommers. He was just like me, wild and free, until he decided to settle down. Got hitched up to a gal from Kansas. Big strappin' gal, taller'n stronger'n he was. Then the children started comin,' and that's when somethin' changed and Abner weren't the same man as before."

Chalmers shakes his head in consternation, stuffs the pipe into the pocket of his buckskin jacket, and folds his hands behind his head. "You set your feet down long enough in one place and they'll grow roots just like a tree. Then you forget everything you learned about livin' on your own and you stop thinkin' the way a man was meant to think."

Tom considers Chalmers' words. "So what become of your partner?"

"Dunno. S'pose he's bouncin' grandkids on his knee by now. Not the kinda life I like to consider. But then everybody's different."

"Amen to that," adds Tom. "I 'spect we're entitled to make damn fools of ourselves if that's our pleasure. But any damned fool gotta admit that eatin' fresh caught trout under the shade on a river bank sure beats..."

Chalmers suddenly sits up straight. He raises his hand, hushing Tom. He twists his head from one side to another, his eyes darting this way and that. He sits motionless, listening, then glances at his mule. Elmer's ears stand straight up. His big, angular head is pointed upriver, nose testing the air.

Chalmers gets to his feet, staring upriver, his head cocked to listen. "They's somebody comin'. We best take cover—fast!"

Tom scrambles up. He breaks the fishing line off the willow branch, rolls the line quickly into a ball and plunges it, hook and all, into his shirt. He slings his saddle onto the chestnut and pulls the cinch tight. All the while his eyes are upriver, his ears cocked.

Chalmers kicks the ashes and fish bones into the river. He mounts and rides through the current, which is up to the withers on his mule. Tom swings up on the chestnut, snatches up the lead rope to the packhorse, and follows, his hand on the stock of the rifle in his leather scabbard.

Once across the river, Chalmers dismounts behind a tall willow thicket, not far from the bank. He motions Tom to do the same. A clattering of hooves resounds a hundred yards upriver and a string of horses and riders soon appear through the willows.

Chalmers squints and studies them. "Mountain Utes," he whispers, pulling his rifle from its scabbard and holding it across his chest. Chalmers silently cocks the hammer.

They stand well hidden and silent, watching the riders approach. Tom gently pulls the bay to him and quietly slides his rifle from the scabbard. He cranes his head to study the riders through the hatch work of willow canes. There are fifteen braves. They move at a fast trot along the opposite riverbank.

The lead rider suddenly reins in his pony and sniffs the air. He motions the others to stop. The braves draw rein and their horses dance noisily on the river cobbles. The braves are clad in buckskin breeches, their hair worn in long braids. They carry rifles across their arms. Some wear sheath knives, others have cudgels dangling from their belts. They are well-muscled and young.

The lead rider studies the ground and notices the smear of ashes and scuff marks. He raises his eyes and scans the willows across the river where Tom and Chalmers stand. Chalmers gently fingers the trigger of his rifle. His breathing is slow and quiet. Tom feels sweat bead up on his scalp. His breathing is fast and shallow. His hands tremble as he cradles his rifle.

The lead rider, a thin, lithe, muscular man, grunts and gestures across the river, his eyes studying the willow thicket. He swings his pony around, nudging it with his heels. The horse plunges in and Chalmers shifts his rifle. When the rider's horse is knee-deep in the current, a hawk screeches from somewhere upstream. The rider quickly reins in his pony, looking upriver. Another screech floats on the air. The leader grunts a few guttural sounds, glances once more across the river, then turns his horse and trots back to join his band. With a wave to the others, he sets off at a fast trot. The others converge on his trail, several of them glancing behind them.

"Damnation!" sighs Tom, "That was too clo..."

Chalmers waves him silent, still looking upriver. Soon, a lone Ute comes up at a fast trot. This man is older than the others, sitting his horse erect and noble. He is tall and heavily built. His nearly naked body shows scars of battles fought long ago. He holds a rifle across his deep chest and wears only a loin cloth. Chalmers peers though the willows.

"Well, I'll be..." he whispers.

The rider stops at the cottonwood and studies the ground. He notices the ashes, then raises his head and casts his glance across the river. He tests the air with his nose, sniffs fast and deep. He cocks his head to listen, then swivels to look up valley. He glances again at the willows, then presses his knees into his mount and canters after the others. His hoof beats fade into silence. Soon, only the gentle hiss of the river remains.

Tom and Chalmers are silent. Satisfied, the old man carefully lowers the hammer and slips his rifle back into its scabbard. "Sure as I'm born that was Colorow; chief of the Mountain Utes."

"Who's Colorow?" demands Tom.

"Never mind that now. We best ride before them Injuns change their minds and come back lookin' for us. They's something upriver they don't like. Let's find out what it is."

Chalmers mounts the mule and Tom swings up on the chestnut. He tugs on the lead rope and draws the packhorse close. They push upstream through the willows along the riverbank until a rock outcrop forces them to cross. They ride half a mile to where the river twists sharply north.

Chalmers suddenly puts up his hand and reins in the mule. Tom draws up on the chestnut. Chalmers listens, then motions them toward a stand of oak brush on a narrow bench above the river. Acorns are just forming on the branches amid deep green leaflets. They dismount and lead the mule and the horses through the oaks and onto the bench where they get themselves well hidden in the brush. Chalmers pulls out his rifle. Tom does the same.

The sound of horses floats down the river. When they get closer, Chalmers lowers his rifle and slips it back into its scabbard. "Soldiers," he says.

"How do you know?" whispers Tom, his eyes riveted toward the sound.

"Shoes," says Chalmers calmly. "Steel shoes."

Chalmers takes up the reins and guides his mule back to the river, where he mounts, waiting. Tom remains in the oak brush, nervously clutching his rifle. Soon, a column of cavalry arrives, twenty soldiers in single file, led by a young lieutenant who raises his gloved hand and halts the troops behind him.

"Howdy," greets Chalmers, his hand in the air.

The officer rides up to the old man and studies him.

"How'd you get past them injuns?"

"What injuns?" asks Chalmers, putting on a deadpan face.

The lieutenant turns to the sergeant behind him. "Flannery, take the men and follow the trail."

The sergeant swings his horse around Chalmers, glances at the old man, and waves on the men. The soldier's faces are stern and tense; they ride with eager purpose. Once the troops have passed, the lieutenant gazes at Chalmers with suspicion.

"You some kind 'a injun trader or what?"

"I'm just a man mindin' his own business, not wantin' no trouble with nobody."

"Well, the Utes don't feel the same. Be better off when they're all dead and gone."

Chalmers remains silent, his gaze diverted to the river.

"Where you comin' from?"

"Brown's Hole," mumbles Chalmers, swallowing his distaste for the cocky officer.

"Travelin' alone?"

"Yep, that's right."

"Well, you best watch yourself," warns the lieutenant. "They's trouble brewin'."

"Much obliged," says Chalmers tersely.

The lieutenant spits into the river, glances once more at Chalmers, taps the brim of his hat and rides off. Chalmers watches him go, then glances up into the brush. "You can come out'a there now," he hollers.

Tom slowly leads the horses through the brush. At the river he swings up into his saddle, then stands in the stirrups looking downstream to make sure the soldiers are gone. The old man looks him over. "Just what're you hidin' from, boy?"

Tom meets Chalmers' gaze without flinching. "I've taken to hidin' from most everyone, old man. A fella can live longer that way."

"Maybe you got somethin' there."

"Came to me in a moment of contemplation," says Tom with a smile.

"I'll make a philosopher out 'a you yet," grins the old man.

At camp that night in a circle of tall pines Tom props himself up against a log and Chalmers sits cross-legged on a thick bed of pine duff. The flickering firelight illuminates his creased, bearded face. The old man puffs his pipe into a red glow and lets the smoke seep from his mouth.

"Why'd you lie to them soldiers?" asks Tom.

"Guess I don't like soldiers much."

"Whyn't you shoot that Ute? He was alone. You could'a got away with it."

"He weren't harmin' me," Chalmers reasons. "Way I look at it, killing a man is like killing a part of yourself. It's a debt you can never repay."

"You kill anybody before?"

The old man puffs a cloud of smoke from his pipe and stares into the fire. "I killed men, but I don't rightly know how many. In the war I fed grapeshot into a cannon like I was feedin' some crazed animal. When that gun went off, men fell, sometimes whole lines of 'em. After the war, I come west and killed Injuns, but I didn't really figure they was humans until I served under Chivington at Sand Creek." He shakes his head. "That man was a murderer and I done his killin' for him...women, children, old men. What I seen at Sand Creek..." Chalmers takes in a deep breath and lets out a sigh. "That's when I begun to feel shame, the shame of bein' a man."

"You feel shame for killin' injuns?"

Chalmers pauses. "You can't blame Injuns for the way they live because it's how they been raised for thousands of years. But the whites mean to get rid of 'em because they want what the Injuns got. So there's a war, and the Injuns are gonna lose sure as we're sittin' here. Their way of live is over. And one day, Tom, so will yours and mine. One day there aint gonna be room enough for the likes of us."

The last flickers of the fire burn down to a tiny blue tongue of flame that licks over a pine knot. Cool air pushes silently into the fire ring where the men stare mutely at the glowing coals. Tom lies back on his blanket and wraps his canvas slicker around him. He gazes up at the stars, musing over what Chalmers has said, thinking about his place in all this, then he rolls to his side and closes his eyes. Sleep comes quickly, and soon he is breathing in a slow, steady, peaceful rhythm.

Chalmers sits straight and still. He listens to the distant sigh of wind moving through the trees. He feels a sense of ease with his life and the way he looks at the world. His left hand tingles, but he ignores it, just as he ignores a pain in his chest that has been swelling for the past few days. His wonder is focused on what stretches beyond the here and now. He pictures the Ute paradise of rivers overflowing with fish, of meadows crowded with game, of tall trees swaying in the wind, of blue skies and warm sunshine, of strong braves and beautiful women, of life in a world of plenty where horses graze in deep green grass and there is no war, where all men are brothers and Manitou smiles down from a mountaintop, blessing it all. He wonders if Manitou can recognize him as a good man. He wonders if he has earned a place in the Ute paradise.

The next day they contour across a series of dry shale flats where the smell of sage wafts up around them, strong in the hot sun. They drop into a lush valley and ford a swollen river where the water is deep and cold and fast. Most of their gear gets wet, so they spread out their bedrolls over sun-warmed river rocks. Tom casts in his line and pulls in a trout while Chalmers rests in the shade of a tall spruce.

"What's on your mind, old man?" asks Tom as he roasts the fish on a willow over a fire. "When we partnered up at Brown's Hole, you said you had a place in mind. Where you leadin' us, anyway?"

"To my paradise," smiles Chalmers. "I told you 'bout my sacred valley, the place where gold and silver are there for the takin' and wild game is everywhere. I'm old and tired, son, and that's the place for me to winter over, maybe last out my days. You with me?"

"Aint no way I'm gonna pass up a man's paradise when he's so kindly offered it," smiles Tom.

The men ride into the evening up the big river valley until it narrows into a canyon with towering walls of yellow sandstone. Tom follows the old man and his mule as they cut out of the valley and head south over scrub-covered hills, then east again where the land ramps gently up into a vast aspen forest threaded with well-beaten game trails, cut with creeks and steep gullies, and interspersed with flowery meadows. The woods are alive with birdsong. Tall mountains rise in every direction, snow-capped and gleaming. Tom cranes his neck for a view, thrilled by the sight of an untracked wilderness that seems to go on forever.

"Up over yonder is my paradise," says Chalmers, reining in his mule and pointing to a high saddle between two peaks where storm clouds gather, dark and foreboding. "We'll cross her in the morning."

Ravens cackle overhead while the men set up camp at the edge of an aspen grove near a small, sparkling stream. Chalmers calls back with a cackle so raven-like that the birds swoop in for a look. As they unsaddled their mounts, Tom notices Chalmers favoring his left arm.

"Got a bad wing, old man?"

Chalmers has been trying to avoid the appearance of a handicap, but his left arm has become progressively numb until he can hardly use it. There is tightness in his chest that makes his breathing short. He feels like there's an anvil crushing his ribs. He is lightheaded most of the time.

"I'll be okay. Just need some rest, a bit of grub, and a good pipe. I'll be fine."

Chalmers stretches out on his bedroll. His left arm is useless, and he wonders if he can make it over the pass in the morning. This brings on a tremor of anxiety as he realizes that old age means the loss of many of his cherished freedoms and that philosophical musings can only take a man so far as a comfort to the many trials of his life. He glances toward the mountain pass where the sun gleams, and he determines to make the crossing the next day.

Tom covertly studies Chalmers. He notices that his complexion has changed from ruddy red to ashen gray. Tom gathers wood and lights a fire with flint and steel. He dips water into a pot from the creek and sets it alongside the flames. Chalmers stirs when the water is ready. He places a pinch of herbs from his worn leather pouch into the steaming pot, which produces a pungent aroma. Chalmers sips the hot drink from a gourd while Tom takes up his rifle and walks off into the woods; all of this without a word spoken. In the dim light of dusk, Chalmers hears a distant shot. Tom arrives in the last filtering light with a flank of venison slung over his shoulder.

"I'll get the rest in the mornin'," assures Tom, who skewers strips of venison on a sharpened willow spit and roasts them over the coals until they are succulent and bubbling with juice. Tom gorges, but the old man doesn't eat.

"Somethin's got a hold 'a me and it aint lettin' go," mumbles Chalmers.

He leans against his saddle, cradling his left arm and gazing at the flames. The pipe remains in his pocket and his conversation is short. Chalmers can feel his heartbeat throbbing in his head, and it beats with a crazy rhythm. Without a word, the old man turns on his side. He falls in and out of sleep until dawn, crazy dreams spinning through his mind.

In the morning, Tom helps Chalmers saddle his mule. The old man is unable to use his left arm and it hangs listlessly at his side. The left side of his face droops and twists his mouth at a downward angle.

"Son, I'll be needin' your help climbin' up on old Elmer," says Chalmers, his voice slurred and bereft of his usual lightness. His eyes are opaque and watery. There is a somber quality to his actions, a studied, disciplined effort, even for the easiest tasks.

Tom effortlessly boosts the old man into the saddle and steadies him, surprised by how thin and light the old man is. Chalmer's breathing is raspy and shallow, his vitality sapped, his expression pained.

"You sure you wanna press on, Chalmers? We could make a mighty nice camp right here, and there's game aplenty."

Chalmers glances down at Tom. "Up there. That's the only place I wanna be. You go fetch that meat...catch me on the pass." Chalmers forces a smile, then kicks the mule into a walk.

Tom watches Chalmers sway precariously in the saddle. He decides not to go after the meat, but to keep pace with his partner. He hurriedly loads the packhorse, then swings into the saddle and follows the old man and the mule.

They climb through thick timber along a network of game trails. When the timber thins at tree-line, the way becomes steep over loose rock. Chalmers keeps to the saddle and coaxes the mule while Tom walks his horses up through the rocky basin. Above them are jutting peaks that surround them on all sides. When Tom reaches the pass, Chalmers sits his mule, hunched over as if there is a big weight on his shoulders. His face is contorted and he wears a twisted smile as he stares down into a wide green basin hemmed in with rock spires and cliff bands that form the lip of the basin like the broken rim of a teacup. A small lake, circled with aspens, sparkles in the sun.

"Aint she pretty," growls Chalmers through clenched teeth.

His statement is answered by a muffled explosion somewhere in the timber below, then by another. Chalmers stiffens. He studies the basin where several puffs of smoke emanate from a clearing half a mile below the highest band of timber. "I'll be a son-of-a-bitch," he says, and nudges the mule forward.

They follow switchbacks on a faint track across the basin where wildflowers bloom and springs burble into a braid of streams running fresh and clear. As they cross the basin another explosion rents the stillness and spooks their mounts. A cloud of dust and smoke rises out of the lower valley.

They wend their way through huge spruce and fir, then come into a clearing. Chalmers halts his mule and Tom draws up next to him. Before them, sloping gently down, is a long, verdant meadow. At the far end of the meadow, half a mile away, stands a cluster of half a dozen white tents. Pack animals are picketed at regular intervals. Several men swing axes, notching logs for a cabin, which stands several courses high. The sound of their chopping is rhythmic and hollow. A harnessed team of mules pulls into the meadow driven by a man walking behind with long reins in his hands. The mules are skidding logs into the clearing. Another blast echoes across the meadow and a large puff of smoke billows from a rocky ridge where several men scurry about with shovels and picks. Their unintelligible voices float across the distance.

Chalmers, clutching his bad arm to his side, surveys the camp with dread. "They done found my paradise," he mourns, shaking his head in disbelief. Chalmers turns his mule back up into the basin. Tom follows without a word. As they thread their way back up through the big trees another explosion rents the air.

Chalmers, slumped over in his saddle, guides his mule to a cleft in a low rock ledge where a faint trail cuts between a matching pair of towering spruce. Squirrels chatter in the treetops as the men ride into a circle of enormous trees. A fire ring is in the center. A lodgepole pine is lashed horizontally between two of the trees.

"Help me down," implores Chalmers, his eyes half closed.

Tom guides the old man to a sheltered hollow between two of the biggest trees. The boughs interlock overhead, forming a natural roof. The ground is soft with duff and the air is fragrant with earthy musk. Tom arranges Chalmers' bedroll and the old man reclines stiffly against a flat boulder. Tom unsaddles the mule and covers Chalmers with the tattered woolen blanket. The old man closes his eyes and appears to doze. Tom unsaddles his mount and unloads the packhorse. He sits quietly before Chalmers, watching him. Chalmers' eyelids flutter as he struggles to focus on Tom. His voice comes in a husky whisper.

"I won't be ridin' out of this basin, Tom, and it's here I want you to leave me. Take Elmer with you and leave me here, but not underground. Just lay me out where Manitou can find me and take me on home."

"You need some herbs, that's all," assures Tom. "I'll get a fire goin' and make up some of that tonic. You and me'll ride out of here in a few days. Maybe them fellas down there got some medicine that'll fix you up."

"No!" growls Chalmers. "I don't want nothin' from them. It's just you and me, Tom, just like it's been since we joined up at Brown's Hole."

That evening, after the sun drops over the ridge, Chalmers drifts off. His mouth gapes open. His breathing becomes dry and raspy.

Tom gathers wood and lights a fire. He fills the pot from a trickle in the rocks and sets it by the flames. He rummages through Chalmers' bags and finds the medicine pouch. He makes a brew, but the old man fails to respond to Tom's gentle nudging. Not even the steaming gourd held under his nose brings him to. His breathing is halting. Sometimes it stops altogether. When it stops, Tom stops breathing, too. When the old man starts up again, Tom commences. They breathe together for some hours. At dark, as the first stars glint through the tree canopy, a gurgling sound comes from Chalmers' lungs with each struggling breath.

Tom sits by the fire watching Chalmers, who lies still, his lungs working fewer and fewer breaths, the gurgling rising up into his throat and causing him to choke and sputter. The old man's face is like a mask, stretched and taut, his mouth gaping to one side, his yellow teeth exposed. He looks waxen and very old, and when Tom touches his hand, the skin feels brittle and cool. When his last labored breath is made and the silence lasts, Tom kneels down and studies him. He gently folds back the blanket and presses his ear to the old man's chest. There is no sound, no beating of the aged heart. Tom wraps Chalmers in the woolen blanket. He sits before him while the fire dies and the night breezes blow and the stars circle and the Earth spins through space.

A man is a man, thinks Tom, reciting what Chalmers has told him. He lives by values and he lives by dreams, but no amount of contemplation or philosophizing is going to stop the hand of death from its rightful due. In the end, man is just another animal, subject to the same laws of nature that rule every living thing.

Tom feels the stillness of the night more acutely than ever before. He savors it without sleep, and he watches the dawn come with a new appreciation for the gift of life, for the rhythm of the days, the weeks, the months, the years. He wonders about his own death and hopes to do as well as Chalmers; to pass away in a place where the wind can carry his soul among the mountains to the realm of whatever god he chooses, into whatever image of heaven he might conceive. Maybe that's how it ends, he muses: heaven is an individual construct awaiting each of us in turn.

In the full light of morning, Tom stands before Chalmers. Propped up on the boulder, his blanket wrapped around him, the old man's face is contorted but strangely placid, his spirit having flown in the night. Tom stacks rocks around the corpse to form a crude ring, an open tomb, where the old, discarded body will gradually be received by nature, broken down to its elemental parts.

Tom loads the packhorse and ties the lead rope to his saddle. He snags the mule's halter rope and leads Elmer towards the big meadow, where he mounts up and nudges the chestnut into a walk. The mule balks and jerks back with his big, angular head. Tom turns and tugs the lead, but the mule wouldn't budge.

"Come on, Elmer," sighs Tom, pulling again on the rope. "Leave the old man to his peace."

The mule jerks back, harder this time, tugging the rope out of Tom's hand. Elmer trots back into the clearing and stands before Chalmers. He paws the ground before the circle of rocks.

Tom dismounts and walks back to the mule. He attempts to lead him out, but the mule won't take a step.

"Okay, Elmer, if this is where you're stayin', then so be it. Keep the old man company, if that's what you want."

Tom removes the mule's halter and Elmer stands guard before his old friend. As Tom turns to leave, the mule nuzzles the old man gently on the cheek. Elmer stomps in distress, pawing the ground. He snorts and blows in confusion.

Tom walks from the clearing, mounts the chestnut, and decides not to visit the camp below. Instead, he rides as high as he can in the basin, then scrabbles his way to the high pass, his horses in tow. From the heights of the ridge, he looks down and locates the circle of trees where the old man lies. Tom touches his shirt pocket, which bulges with the leather herb pouch and the long-stemmed pipe.

Tom watches cloud shadows race across the peaks. His thoughts drift like those clouds as he tries to summon meaning to life and death. He knows Chalmers would appreciate the multitude of philosophical questions rising in his fertile mind. He rues that the old man won't be there to discuss them around a fire with roasted fish and freshly killed game scenting the air, and with the familiar pipe shedding a red glow on the weathered, old face. ☆

Chapter 6 | The Woman Across the Table

I T WAS A QUIET AUTUMN DAY when Rebecca Wilson strolled into the deserted foyer of Paepcke Auditorium. She stood for a moment and took in the silence. She peered discreetly into the small, octagonal library and sniffed the smell of old books and stale air. She looked into the art gallery where hung canvasses bearing sharp lines, cubes, trapezoids, blocks of color. She tiptoed across the carpet and studied a wall of photographic portraits of prominent men and women—the lineage of the Aspen Institute.

Furtively, she opened the auditorium door and gazed into the darkness. She thought of Plato's cave as her shadow loomed over rows of empty seats. She left the building and stepped out into the shaded courtyard. There stood a bust of Mortimer Adler, the ponderous skull atop narrow shoulders. The wall of the Koch building bore curious markings from Herbert Bayer, and she wondered if the ragged lines etched into the stucco were disguising cracks in the facade.

Now that she was in Aspen, Rebecca wondered why. The seminar scholarship was a nice gift and acknowledgement, but it wasn't that alone. Musing in the courtyard, she confessed to herself that Aspen was yet another proving ground for her, that she was lured here by a kind of intellectual gamesmanship. The Executive Seminar was her opportunity to challenge the ethics and morality of the accepted wisdom of the ages, which she found both outmoded and unjust.

She pushed open the door to the seminar building, which was also empty and hushed. She found the placard announcing her seminar and entered an octagonal room with an octagonal table surrounded by swivel chairs. Around the table were place cards, notepads, water pitchers, and small dishes filled with hard candies. Rebecca found her name card and settled into her chair. She rolled gently on its castors and was getting a feel for the room when the door swung open and a man entered.

Stan Foster's decision to attend the seminar was not his. Three days after his father's death, only a month before, Stan Jr. was summoned to the office of his Uncle Jerome, the CEO of Foster & Sons, whose Chicago law offices occupied several floors of a century-old Gothic office building on LaSalle Street.

"Stanley, your father's will is a bit unusual," announced Jerome from behind his colossal mahogany desk. "He has left you in charge of his estate, and a management role in the firm, but there is a condition. Your father made it clear that before you assume these responsibilities you must 'broaden your perspective.' These are his exact words," said Jerome, indicating the document on his desk. "Your father felt very strongly about his experiences over the years at the Aspen Institute, and he insisted that you should have the same exposure. The Executive Seminar, therefore, will become part of your training."

Stan groaned his objection, to which Uncle Jerome shrugged. "I can't say I always understood my brother's interest in Aspen, but it was one of his passions. Anyway, it's not open for debate; the will makes it very clear. You will attend the seminar before any further conveyance of your father's estate. In the meantime, I will serve as executor."

Stan's father had come to Aspen with the original wave of executives in the fifties. He gave generously to the Institute's endowment and discovered an engaging battleground in the Adler-led seminars. It was Mortimer Adler, the architect of the seminar, who had defined the two competing triads at work in the world: The Platonic triad, representing the good, the true, and the beautiful; and the Machiavellian triad, representing money, fame and power.

Stanley Foster Sr., whose picture hung on the wall in Paepcke Auditorium, knew in which of the triads he reigned. Machiavelli was his patron saint, and during seminars he thundered support for the market-driven sagacity of Milton Friedman, his exemplar for pure capitalism.

Stanley Sr. attended the Executive Seminar every three years as atonement for his confessed bottom-line myopia, and he was always given the part of King Creon in the requisite production of "Antigone." So accustomed did he become to that tragic role that among fellow Institute trustees he bore the sobriquet "KC". Clad in crown and toga in the marble garden, he strutted the grassy stage and spoke his lines with magisterial conviction. He never understood why Creon was so maligned, seeing him in metaphor as a wronged CEO whose exercise of executive authority had been in the best interests of the family kingdom. In his later years, "KC" was able to recite Creon's lines from memory, which elicited awe and occasional chuckles from seminar novitiates.

Stanley Foster Sr. felt invigorated under the withering demands of Adler. He took occasional scolding from the supreme moderator, enduring them like an intellectual flogging. He felt it was in the best interests of family and firm that Stanley Jr., his only son, should endure the same crucible and emerge with whatever glimmer of pained enlightenment might arise from a forced feeding of the Great Books of Western Civilization. To Stanley Sr., the intellectual high ground provided a loftier vantage from which to subject underlings to his indomitable, aristocratic will. It was noblesse oblige that drove him to explore the values-laden principles of leadership, even though he ignored them at critical junctures in his professional life.

Now it was Junior's turn to face the demands of the Aristotelian world, to lift himself from the lockstep cadence of the firm and embrace the vaunted Aspen tradition. When a boxy package arrived in the mail a fortnight after his meeting with Uncle Jerome, Stan Jr. tore it open and hefted the seminar readings notebook with a grimace. It was the size of the Sunday *New York Times*. He read with misgivings the opening missive: "For one week you will detach from your everyday life to examine and reflect on fundamental issues and values... It's extremely important that you read the texts... The seminar will stay with you not merely as a memory, but as an active part of your life." But I've already got a life, and a damned good one, thought Stan.

Stan arrived in Aspen on an early flight, so he checked into his room and wandered the Meadows campus. Put out by what he rued as an interruption in his demanding life, he was annoyed at being removed from the buffering din of the city and the hectoring pace of the firm, both of which fed his nervous energy. He had skimmed the readings, grudgingly, and now the notion of five days of discussion left him enervated and a little out of sorts. He did not wish to examine his values or any other values, thank you, and he resented his forced consent to the seminar. The one thing he found refreshing was the liberty of being on his own, free of domestic obligations, away from the constant chatter of his wife and children, absent from the gravitational pull of the family manse on the tree-shaded bluff overlooking Lake Michigan in suburban Winnetka.

Stan Jr. spent half an hour in the Meadows health club hot tub gazing at the opulent real estate on Red Mountain. He pedaled an exer-cycle until it bored him. He showered, dressed and followed the walkway past the grassy knolls, which made him think of Dallas and JFK. He glanced across at the mountains and found them too imposing for his sense of what nature ought to be. He began exploring the old haunts of his father until he pulled open the door of the seminar room and found a black woman sitting at the table. The room was dim because no lights were on, so it took him a moment to see her in the gloom. She glanced up at him with a look of surprise, a flash of eyes.

"Hello!" she said.

"Oops! Sorry. S'cuse me," he stammered, turning to leave.

"No bother." She was quickly on her feet, following him out the door.

"You in the seminar?" he asked as they faced each other in the hallway.

"Yes," she nodded. "Hi, I'm Rebecca." She extended her hand.

"Oh, hi, I'm Stan, Stan Foster." They shook hands and walked together toward the door.

"Got the readings down?"

"I think so," she smiled.

"Well, see you tonight."

At the reception dinner Stan Foster and Rebecca Wilson smiled and nodded at one another as they sipped cocktails with the others who would share the seminar table. The small talk bored Stan, so he fled after the perfunctory introductions, which reminded him of opening day at summer camp in Wisconsin.

Rebecca was equally uneasy, realizing that she was the only person of color in the room. She made polite conversation, wondering if the intellectual power of the other participants would be worthy of the time she'd spent on the readings. She suddenly felt over-prepared.

Stan slept fitfully and was groggy in the morning. The weak coffee at breakfast didn't begin to cut his mental fog. In his room he brushed his teeth, applied an extra smear of underarm deodorant, and studied himself in the mirror for errant nose and ear hairs. He prodded his midsection with his fingers and tried sucking in the paunch that had mysteriously morphed his once youthful physique into stodgy middle age. Still, for a mature man in his 40s, he was satisfied with his appearance in striped collared shirt, creased khaki pants, and tasseled loafers. Stan gathered his readings and shambled reluctantly to the seminar room.

Rebecca was up early and, after a solitary breakfast in a corner of the Meadows restaurant, during which she perused the *New York Times*, she strolled the manicured grounds, taking in the cool mountain air. She dressed for the casual atmosphere of the seminar, as the instructions recommended, wearing slacks and a loose-fitting sweater that felt appropriate to the mountains.

Stan and Rebecca nearly bumped into one another at the door of the seminar room, which Stan held open and invited her passage with a gallant sweep of his arm. Soft chatter greeted them as they entered. Gathered at the table was a school teacher from Virginia, a CPA from Boston, a chemist from New York, an IT entrepreneur from Los Angeles, a hotel manager from DC, a business executive from Baltimore, an interior designer from San Diego, a librarian from Chicago, an oil speculator from Dallas, and a banker from Detroit. Each had their notebook of readings on the table along with their name cards, and each wore nametags dangling on blue strings around their necks.

The moderator, a learned professor from a small, prestigious college in Oregon, stood up and rang a large brass bell that elicited titters from the participants. Stan felt like one of Pavlov's dogs. "I would like to begin by pointing out the words of Oliver Wendell Holmes," said the moderator, gesturing to a poster on the wall behind him. He read with theatrical verve: "'A man's mind once stretched beyond its normal dimensions never returns to its original size.'" He looked around the room as the gravity of the statement settled in. "Let's see if Mister Holmes is right. Please open your books to *The Republic*, by Plato.

The discussion got off slowly as the participants balked at the questions contrived by the moderator. Only Rebecca Wilson was engaged from the start, eager to establish herself as a player. Her voice was strong, her words clear, her bearing powerful. She had studied the readings, and the force of her intellect was irrepressible. Here was a powerful woman, a rare creature, thought Stan. Given the intellectual passivity of his usual circle of friends and family, there was something refreshing about her. By afternoon, churning through Aristotle, Hobbes, and Rousseau, Rebecca was clearly the star, a brilliant beacon that illuminated every point she touched.

The moderator strove to conceal his satisfaction, but he smiled in spite of himself. Rebecca Wilson was the kind of participant that made it all worthwhile—informed, opinionated, impassioned, articulate. This is what brought meaning to the dialogue and stirred life into the written word. The other seminarians remained mostly reticent. None could touch her mastery of the texts, her quick analyses, her easy eloquence, so they sat on the sidelines volunteering occasional quips to the moderator's most obvious queries. Most of them, including Stan, found it convenient and edifying to let Rebecca do all the heavy lifting.

Stan Foster counted the seconds, the minutes, the hours. He hadn't endured such tedium since college. The Greeks were passé, he concluded, so why dredge them up? Some of the texts were purposefully obfuscating, so why bother sorting them out? As for Rebecca Wilson, she was a show off, a teacher's pet.

But as he sat there, enduring a swarm of ideas from her fertile mind, something gradually awoke in him. The force of Rebecca's intellect, coupled with the fluidity of her words, the choice of her vocabulary, and the accuracy of her diction, began to strike him with her every word. By the end of the day he couldn't take his eyes off her, drawn there by the magnetism of her energy and confidence. Stan was shocked to feel such an attraction to this woman's vital mind and to realize how she made him feel slightly inferior. The men of the Foster family were not calibrated for inferiority, and the mere suggestion of it chafed him.

Rebecca had decided that no matter what the composition of the group, she would assert herself with her mastery of the readings. By establishing herself as an authority on the texts, she could weigh in later with her agenda, which was denouncing the haughty pretense of what she identified as the "Aspen Establishment." The wealth and privilege on conspicuous display here inflamed her sense of social justice and empowered her egalitarian zeal. Throughout the advanced stages of her education she had felt a duty to better the elites at their own game. Now she would do so on their own turf, the so-called "Athens of the West."

For dinner that night they climbed into vans and drove up a snaking mountain road to an old lodge surrounded by ragged mountain peaks. After a catered meal they gathered around a roaring campfire on the edge of a meadow where dramatic ridgelines were silhouetted in a starry sky. A young man with long hair and a wispy beard, the resident naturalist, told them about the geological drama of glacial carving and the habitat nuances of mule deer, elk, and beavers. Rebecca wondered what all of this nature infusion had to do with the world of ideas, but wrote it off as quaint local color. Stan was tired and restless and wished he were back in Chicago. He drank down his glass of wine and stared into the hypnotic flames. Summer camp, indeed. The other participants exulted in these wild and rustic surroundings, but Stan and Rebecca unknowingly shared a less idealized view of the wilderness backdrop. To them, it was a distraction from the important agendas of their lives.

On Day Two, Rebecca's composure cracked and exposed the bleeding heart within. She vented on Milton Friedman and his paean to the free market. She dismissed with hostility Plato's defense of slavery. She questioned the sagacity of the dead white males responsible for many of the seminar texts. She subtly chastised the others at the table for what she saw as the complacency of their silence. Her pent up animosity rushed in a poetic flood of words that burned with outrage as she grieved for the lost potential of humanity. Her anger caused her voice to quaver.

"Friedman!" She jabbed her finger on the open notebook before her. "He says on page 245, line 2, and I quote: 'The typical state of mankind is tyranny, servitude, and misery.' It's clear that Friedman has taken his cue from Hobbes, who said that life without a Leviathan is solitary, poor, nasty, brutish and short." She slammed shut her notebook and strafed the room with her eyes. "Hobbes and Friedman echo the same truth. The free market is a wilderness in which there is no Leviathan other than the market—no ethic other than greed—no coercive power other than fear. Greed and fear—that's what makes the market tick and that's why the fundamentals of American capitalism are corrupt."

Rebecca sat back in her chair, her eyes on fire as they swept the room, daring anyone to challenge her. Stan arched his eyebrows, twisted his pen in his hand, felt his blood pressure rise. Rebecca was playing hardball and he didn't even have a bat. Something awakened in Stan's psyche. A force was germinating in the Hobbesian world Rebecca had just described. He felt the brute in him rising up angry.

"Okay," cut in the moderator, "but Friedman also states that a CEO should not step outside his corporate role and pursue altruism or charity with the resources of his company when it's not part of his job description. Is this sound reasoning?"

"No!" said Rebecca emphatically, "because every institution comprising a social order, private or public, should be concerned with the welfare of that society. The corporation must have accountability beyond the boardroom, beyond shareholder earnings, beyond the profit motive. Accountability must come from inside," she thumped her chest, "from a moral and ethical bearing...from the heart!"

Rebecca was suddenly out of breath. She felt a wave of emotion surging through her. Reaching for her water glass, she couldn't keep her hand from shaking. She had vowed not to let herself go quite so far, so fast, and now the genie was out of the bottle, the taboo of emotional control was broken.

The air was so still that Stan could hear the rustle of aspen leaves fluttering in the courtyard. He suddenly took a very personal interest in the seminar. This was no longer passive entertainment. "Rebecca!" His voice boomed across the room. "You denounce the free market, the same free market that has underwritten the material comforts of the American lifestyle, the same free market that has rescued millions of people from poverty. You share the fruits of that system and yet you denigrate it. What Hobbes was saying, is that without a Leviathan, all men are at war against all other men. You prove that here because you're fighting your own war in this room. Is there no Leviathan ruling you?"

Rebecca's mouth dropped open. She felt like she'd been hit by a two-by-four. "Whoa!" waved down the moderator, who felt a growing, perhaps irreconcilable, intensity in the room that he somehow had to rein in and redirect. "Okay. Good. We're cooking now. Hobbes and Friedman... good connection. Let's keep exploring the links, bringing in other points of view." He glanced at his watch. "Guys, we're out of time. Let's revisit some of these ideas after lunch. We start up at one-thirty. Thank you for a great morning."

Stan Foster sat in his chair as the others filed out. When Rebecca passed behind him, he felt an electric tension that seemed to stand his hair on end. Gerry, the prominent oil man from Dallas, winked and patted him knowingly on the shoulder. Stan sat fuming, not only at Rebecca's outburst, but at his own. Now he was involved. The woman across the table had rattled him, had jangled a nerve. She was shaking his bones, and he didn't like it because the rattle he felt came from his distant past.

Stan had made a dramatic turn when he was at Harvard in the early seventies. He could trace it to the time of the Kent State shootings when he was pulled between revolutionary social idealism and detached self interest. He struggled then with conflicting ideals, but in the end he renounced his emotional urges and embraced the pragmatic path that led him into the family firm. Once he was launched on the career track, he moved like a salmon up a spawning ladder, eventually landing in a big, open pond layered with the silt of convention, the sediment of tradition. Now Rebecca's raw emotional power was stirring up the muck.

Growing up in the Chicago projects, Rebecca had developed a hard edge that cut through the sloganeering of the civil rights era. She witnessed progress for her people, but not enough to assuage her strident sense of injustice. She held her hurt throughout her youth and learned to express it intellectually, with vituperation and brilliant logic. Her adult life was on a collision course with reformist systems and liberal constructs she deemed insufficient to right the grievous wrongs of her people's brutal history.

Walking to his room after the final session that day, the sun soaring magnificently among puffy cumulus clouds, the mountainsides emerald green, Stan realized that his life could have gone elsewhere. But the road less traveled seemed bumpy and weed-grown after college, so he merged in lockstep with the legions treading the paved boulevard. Listening to the woman across the table, and being confronted by her liberal ideals and strident denunciations, he wondered at what cost that decision had been made. He wondered if he had made the decision himself or whether it had been made for him.

Rebecca Wilson's electric current arced to a dormant nerve in Stan's subconscious. That nerve was tingling now with wakefulness. As he walked, he regarded his hulking shadow on the lawn and thought it resembled a Neanderthal. Perhaps his progress in adulthood had been one of devolution, a long, dark regression based upon a cynicism so brutal that it numbed his soul. He wondered if the cynic that ruled him was a phantom guardian that stood against the true message in his heart—the still, small voice. He heard that voice now, loud and clear, and he heard it in her words. His mind was being stretched, uncomfortably and against his will, to the Holmes maxim, and she was stretching it. That night, Stan studied the readings the way he crammed for exams at college. He would be prepared in the morning with the means to refute whatever argument Rebecca might employ to unsettle his embattled psyche.

Day Three opened with a discussion of Martin Luther King's "Letter from the Birmingham Jail." Rebecca rose to her full height, a modern Joan of Arc. The moderator gave her leash because he was just as rapt by her outpouring as were the others. "Reverend King," she spoke the name with solemnity, her voice full of feeling, "knew the risks of his beliefs and his actions, and still he sacrificed himself to his cause. He was the consummate humanist, and he gave everything he had to human dignity..." Her ebony skin gave credence to her summation. "...King was one of the greatest men of the 20th century, perhaps in all of American history. I'm grateful to see this letter in these readings."

Stan thought quickly, desperate for a rejoinder, the cynic clawing for a foothold on a slippery ideological slope. His intellect overruled his honesty and his words boomed like an artillery barrage over the battlefield that he now made of the seminar table. His trajectory was low, his shells incendiary. His target was the woman whose truth stood like a silver standard fluttering in the breeze.

"Reality check!" called out Stan. "You've romanticized King beyond all proportion. This letter is a device, a partial truth. King wrote some of it in jail, that's true, but he spent weeks polishing it later as his manifesto. He knew the importance of a prison screed, and he was opportunistic enough to exploit his jail term for this harangue, just as he used the civil rights movement to advance his own celebrity. King inflamed racial passions and invoked violence that later spread throughout every major American city with a black minority population. King was not a man of peace; he was a revolutionary with a personal political agenda that clearly had Communist overtones. This letter represents a vendetta, his vendetta, which he imposed upon the entire black community."

Rebecca Wilson sat like a statue. Her eyes spoke her hurt and her outrage as she gazed at him from across the table. Her body and mind reeled as the poison of his words coursed through her. No one challenged Stan, not even the abashed moderator. Stan gloated in the hush of the room. Express a position, any position, he reasoned, and you command authority; the stronger the position, the greater the authority. He knew what it was to dominate with bluster and force. Hadn't they discussed Machiavelli just two days before? "You're either on the top or you're on the bottom," his father always told him. "That choice is yours, son."

What amazed Stan Foster most was that he had slandered King without any sense of irony. Only now did he feel the quaking filament in his soul, that quivering fiber of truth that vibrates the way the needle of a lie detector wavers when recording dissonance. King had been his hero, yet he had just slandered the man merely to put Rebecca down. Stan Sr. would have been proud, but Stan Jr. felt a stab of shame.

At lunch he got stuck at a table with Maureen, the interior designer, and Gerry, the oil man. Maureen told him that his ideas were "ponderous," that he gave her "a lot to mull over." Gerry confided with a snicker that it was "terrific to have at least two conservatives in the room." Stan excused himself for a phone call and escaped to his room. He sat on his bed doing something he hadn't done in years, thinking. If King was not his hero, then who was? Stan's loyalty was to the institutions that furthered his ambitions and social prominence—the family, the state, the firm. Rebecca was obviously ruled by passion; he was ruled by...? He feared the answer.

That afternoon, during coffee break, he noticed Rebecca Wilson in the small courtyard behind the seminar building. She sat alone on a low brick wall sipping tea. He got a wild notion and pushed open the glass door. As he approached her, he suddenly realized how beautiful she was, how perfectly poised, like a bronze sculpture.

"Hey," he said with a smile. "I feel I need to explain."

She flashed dark eyes at him. "How dare you utter such blasphemies against Reverend King." She glared at him until he dropped his gaze.

He caught her eyes again, deep brown, clear, unflinching. "Look," he said, "I'd like to believe in ideals and altruism and values, in all the things you talk about. I think I did once when I was young...and probably naïve. But I've been out in the world for a long time and my experience tells me that you can't live that way. Nobody does. It's just not...realistic."

"Then I pity you...you and Machiavelli!" She stood abruptly and faced him, her eyes burning holes through his. "I have never understood you people. I'm trying to, but I haven't gotten there, yet. What happened to you, Stan? When did you give up?" She turned abruptly and walked off across the lawn.

Rebecca hoped in her heart of hearts that Stan was wrong, yet she knew enough not to discount him. She knew of King's dark side, the scandals and adultery, the politics that ruled his life. She worried that great men like King were doomed to flounder in Stan Foster's world of brutal realism, each succumbing to predictable foibles and follies. She wondered if her own ideals were irrational, if she were only fooling herself with her steadfast belief in the good, the true, the beautiful.

Stan felt deflated after Rebecca's rebuff. In the afternoon discussion, he dropped his combative edge. Perhaps he had been too harsh, too aggressive, too forceful. Rebecca was also quiet. Perhaps she had reacted too defensively, too ideologically, too vehemently. Stan studied Rebecca covertly, wondering if he had popped the bubble of her sentimental fantasy world of white knights and good deeds. Rebecca noticed Stan's reticence and felt embarrassed for taking the discussion so personally.

Later, in his room, Stan read the participant bios. Rebecca Wilson:

noted scholar...published poet...sabbatical from Yale...professor of literature...humanitarian activist...married with two children. She was accomplished. She had a family. She walked her talk. Stan's grudging hostility turned to reluctant admiration. There was something about her—an unflinching sincerity—that touched him. She had something that seemed all too rare in his world: authenticity.

In her room, Rebecca Wilson read Stan Foster's bio: Choate... Harvard...debate team...football...trial lawyer...wife...two kids...Winnetka. A child of privilege, she concluded, with the highest education money could buy, a family company to absorb him, a social hierarchy to provide for his every advantage. His upbringing was the antipathy of hers, and yet there was something intriguing about his exalted world and the powerful station he held in it. Rebecca realized she was jousting with a royal prince of the Establishment, and she promised herself that she would take him down.

On Day Four, the moderator took them through the *Analects* of Confucius, a numbered list of truisms that Stan had dismissed as sampler fodder. Discussion lagged, so the moderator primed the pump: "Are there any conclusions we can draw from these *Analects* that bear on our other readings? Do any of them bear on our own lives?"

Rebecca volunteered quietly: "There's one that I think bears on the purpose of this seminar." The moderator nodded for her to continue. "It's *Analect 44.*" Pages were turned. She read: "'To judge others by what one knows of oneself is the method of achieving humanity.'" She sat back and scanned the table for reactions, then settled her eyes on Stan Foster. "What Confucius is saying is that if you want to achieve humanity, all your judgments of others must originate from self-judgment. If you judge by what you know of yourself, you become empathetic. Darwin said that empathy is a fundamental instinct, the root of human ethics. Judging others through ourselves is the most important piece of emotional wisdom we can achieve."

Stan was shaken by her interpretation. As a trial lawyer, he was taught that empathy was a liability. His job was not to feel for the other guy, but to defeat him. Empathy would be the death knell for the legal system, and for capitalism. But if all ethics rest on empathy and empathy is a condition of nature, then what had erased it in him? What kind of life had he been leading that he could perceive empathy as a weakness rather than as a strength? What kind of system was he living under that promoted judgment of others without the balance of self-judgment?

A door creaked open to the long darkened room of his soul and filled it with a blaze of light. Stan could feel his temperature rising, a blush coming to his cheeks. Plato's Cave was suddenly illuminated. The shadows disappeared. For the first time in years, he felt the searing white light of introspection, and it melted through his rigid defenses.

Disoriented, Stan stiffened. He slammed the door shut and shoved home a mental deadbolt against his emotions. He parried her heart thrust with his cynic's sword and lunged for a victor's touch. His synapses fired to his speech mechanism and produced a facile fluidity that surprised even him. He hardly knew what he was saying, but he held his voice calm and followed his instinct. "You're wrong, all wrong." Every eye in the seminar room turned to him. "Empathy is merely a sentiment. Machiavelli would have called it a fault, a fatal flaw. Empathy is a weakness, not a strength. It promotes indecision and capitulation. Self-interest...that's what makes the world go round...not empathy."

The moderator quickly jumped in. "Okay! Confucius to Darwin to Machiavelli. Anyone want to bring in Hobbes, Rousseau, Plato or Friedman?"

No one spoke. This was no longer a seminar; it was a debate between the two of them, between diametrically opposed ideologies, between liberal and conservative, between socialist and capitalist, between woman and man, between right brain and left brain. This was war.

Rebecca glared at Stan. "It's you who have it wrong," she insisted, "because you fail to understand Darwin. He said that even animals feel something for their own kind, which means they have empathy. Empathy represents a connection between souls. Perhaps, Mister Foster, you're ignoring the voice of the soul." Her eyes cut through him like lasers. "Since the soul holds our deepest truths, perhaps you have lost sight of your own truths, or simply choose to deny your soul. Have you no empathy, Mister Foster? Have you no soul?"

Stan's breath caught in his throat. He had no answer, no rejoinder. The door to his psyche was flung open, and this time he couldn't close it. The light came in, and it was her light. His mind raced over bumpy new ground. Soul. Did he even know what soul was? Could he feel it, locate it, describe it? Her expression changed from curiosity to concern as she watched him struggle. Someone coughed. Someone left for the bathroom. The moderator deflected the discussion elsewhere. Rebecca held Stan with her eyes as the empathy she had just described enveloped her. She felt his pain as he twisted and turned in the fires of his personal hell, a hell she had opened for him.

Stan felt his mind race as he groped for reassurance. Had he lost his soul? Is that why he couldn't feel it or identify it? When was the last time he had even considered his soul? Certainly not in church, where he dozed through long-winded sermons. Certainly not at home; he and his wife didn't speak of such things. He had given body and soul to his career. Maybe that's where his soul was—in his office on the eighth floor, tucked into a locked filing cabinet. Had he willingly given away his soul? Didn't everybody in the professional world do that? It was expected of you. Parceling out one's soul is a sign of loyalty, commitment, fealty. In exchange, he was rewarded with raises, bonuses, stock options - all the perks. He had shifted his allegiance from the internal to the external. The still, small voice called out from time to time, nagging from his deepest recesses, but he had learned to filter out the static. That was how he was taught to make it through life, and he was a master of it. Or was he?

When the afternoon discussion ended, Stan Foster was in a fog. As the others filed out, he sat at his place and slowly collected his reading materials. The still, small voice was trying desperately to get his attention. His normal filters—distraction and denial—were not working, so the voice grew into a shrill crescendo that raged through his head until the tumult was overwhelming. He felt his heart racing. Perspiration pricked his scalp. His breathing came fast and shallow. He thought he was having a heart attack.

The last person to leave was the oil man, Gerry, a burly, good-natured sort with a wide face, a bulbous red nose, and a booming voice. Stan could hear the receding voices of the others in the hallway. He hoped Gerry would join them. Stan needed air. He needed to escape the octagonal cement block walls of this suddenly claustrophobic cellblock. He had to see blue sky. Gerry stood blocking the door.

"Pretty hard on you, wasn't she?" said Gerry, shaking his head. "Got a score to settle, that one does. That's the way it is with some of 'em—angry at the world, and especially at the white world. I agree with you, Stan. I think you're right in what you say. I just want you to know I appreciate you speaking your truth."

"Yeah...well...thanks." It was all he could summon without revealing the tremor in his voice, the rising panic. He flipped the ring binder closed and shoved back his chair. He pushed past Gerry and hurried down the hall. "Hey, you all right?" asked Gerry.

Stan Foster felt he was going to be sick. He pushed open the door and hurried out behind the building where he bent over and took several deep breaths. A trail led off through the grass, and he followed the steep pathway down into the river canyon, his loafers slipping on the gravel. The sound of the river beckoned, and he slipped hurriedly down the trail until he entered the cool, deep shade of tall spruce trees. He found his way to the riverbank and stepped onto a smooth granite boulder that sloped to the water's edge. He knelt down and plunged his hands into the cold, clear flow. His hands soon ached from the cold. He pulled them from the water and pressed them against his face. River water mingled with his tears.

A wave of panic surged through him. He was suddenly frightened by the intensity of life, by the surge of doubts that threatened to undermine everything he had done, everything he had been. He felt dizzy as the world spun chaotically, round and round. He opened his eyes and was disoriented by these strange surroundings; river, trees, mountains. Again he dunked his hands into the icy water and pressed them to his face.

Just as the shrieking voice in his head reached a deafening pitch, something deep inside him broke like a dam, flooding him with acceptance. He felt himself relaxing to the sound of the river, to its peaceful hush. He sat back on the sun-baked boulder, took a deep breath, and realized that the future is made by a series of choices, each one a building block to a new life. He was free to choose. He didn't know what to choose, but he felt better for knowing that he was free to remake himself. He took a deep breath and let it out as a slow release of the demons that had possessed him. It was a long time before he climbed back up the hill on the steep, narrow trail, but it was a different man who emerged from the river canyon.

Stan avoided the seminar dinner that night. Instead, he wandered the dark streets of Aspen until his feet ached and his stomach cramped with hunger. When he returned to his room around midnight there was a phone message from the moderator, hoping that Stan was coming to dinner. There was another message from his wife asking for the name of the plumber; a toilet was clogged. He returned neither call. He lay awake in his bed most of the night, his mind too unsettled for sleep. He roused himself at first light, showered, and pulled up a chair to the desk in his room. He took pen to paper and began making a list of vows, ways in which he would change his life. At the head of the list he wrote, "Empathy."

The final day of the seminar began with coffee and rolls at the seminar building. Stan had thought of leaving early, but he decided to face his torments. He was filling his coffee cup as the moderator came into the hallway to ring the morning bell.

"Stan," he said, putting his hand on Stan's shoulder. "We missed you last night."

"Well, something came up."

The moderator looked him in the eyes. "I hope it all got worked out."

"Yeah," said Stan with a nod. "Thanks. Everything's fine."

Stan took his seat and opened his notebook. Rebecca Wilson looked quizzically at him from across the table, probing him with her deep brown eyes. The moderator drew them to Vaclav Havel's essay on transcendence. Stan studied the reading, struggling to focus, his mind dodging elsewhere. He drifted back to the boulder on the edge of the river. He assured himself that the cul-de-sac on which his life had stalled was not a dead end. It had a radius that allowed a turn. He could backtrack down that road. It would mean opening himself to the haunting caverns of his conscience, and for that there would be a price he could not even calculate, possibly the dissolution of everything he had built. As he pondered implausible scenarios, the discussion went on without him.

The moderator broke Stan's contemplation by requesting a moment of meditation on a quote he recited from Martin Luther King, Jr. "We are caught in an inescapable network of mutuality, tied in a single garment of destiny." The moderator gazed around the room. "I want you to consider this statement—not for discussion—just for a few quiet minutes of reflection."

Mutuality. It was a word that Stan Foster had not fully understood before this moment. He wondered if he had ever felt mutuality with anything or anybody, with his wife or his children or his co-workers. Certainly, he had never felt it with his father. Stan recalled how, during a visit home from college, his father had assailed his youthful moralizing as cheap sentiment, dismissed his avowed pacifism as cowardice, ridiculed his sensitivity as weak and effeminate, dispatched his idealism as impractical. In one brutal harangue, his father had crushed Stan's still, small voice. That vision of his father brought back the war, not the one in Vietnam, but the war that had erupted within him after college when he had surrendered utterly to convention. Now the battle for his soul was rejoined, and he recognized that there was still some fight left in him.

For the first time in the seminar, Rebecca Wilson dropped her fists. She allowed King's words to sink in and realized that mutuality was something she had always rejected. She saw clearly how anger ruled her warring world. She felt the sting of her innate hostility, her bitter distrust of humanity. King's voice, the voice she worshiped more than any other, flowed through newly opened channels the way a stamen delivers fertility to a flower. She felt something growing, warm and alive, inside her.

The moderator asked for responses to favorite passages in the notebook. Alice, the school administrator from Cleveland, answered with a reading from Reinhold Niebuhr: "'Only right life is good, and right life is no future ideal but always a present demand.' This quote really appealed to me," said Alice, "because it keeps me on purpose. It makes me focus on everything I do, while I'm doing it."

Stan mused over the notion of the right life, the present demand, concepts that a week ago would have meant nothing, but were now hitting him in the solar plexus. His heart was opening and, like a muscle unused to exercise, it hurt.

The moderator announced that the final half hour would be devoted to closing comments around the table. "I hope you don't mind if we start with you, Rebecca."

Rebecca spoke in her calm poet's voice. "I'd like to refer to Mencius. If there's a good summary for what we've been through, this is it." She studied the page in her notebook and read: "'The sense of compassion is the beginning of humanity; the sense of shame is the beginning of righteousness; the sense of courtesy is the beginning of decorum; the sense of right and wrong is the beginning of wisdom.'" She paused in thought, her eyes raised to the ceiling, studying a cobweb laced in the sunlight. "If we can hold these ideas and if we can weigh these judgments, our lives will reflect the intended outcome, which is the best we can ask for human progress."

The words poured over Stan like hot water over an ice cube. Something in him fractured. He realized with a quickening of his pulse that he would not return to Chicago the same man as when he had left. Something irrevocable had occurred. Life would be different and new. His struggle was just beginning.

When it came his turn, the words came out with spontaneity, surfacing from a deep well. There were no filters and no censors. "I'm a trial lawyer," he confessed. "I defend medical insurance companies against malpractice suits. I've been successful—very successful—without any concern for my opponents. A lot of these people have been hurt, and I hurt them more. I've spent the majority of my adult life in a career that, after all we've read and discussed, seems to be the antipathy of mutuality, empathy, and generosity, all the values in this notebook. I don't know how to reconcile my future with what I'm feeling here, but I intend to try." He swallowed hard and gazed across the table. He locked eyes with Rebecca. "Thank you for pushing me out of my comfort zone and into a place I need to revisit."

Some were embarrassed by his candor, others were teary-eyed. Rebecca shook her head and smiled. And then it was over. People were leaving, saying good-byes. Just as Gerry was approaching, his beefy hand out, Stan Foster scooped up his notebook and hurried from the room. He walked quickly across the campus, relieved to be alone. "Hey, Stan! Wait! I have something for you." He turned. It was Rebecca jogging up behind him. She caught up, breathing hard. Her beauty was radiant from her exertion. She handed him a book.

"I thought you might like this," she smiled.

"Rebecca…" He began, then paused.

"No. Don't." She shook her head. "We said enough…in there. Good-bye and good luck." She backed away, turned, and jogged back toward the seminar building.

In his room, Stan Foster opened the book. It was a collection of Mencius. He paged through it, but there was no inscription, nothing to take with him. At the airport that afternoon, he saw Rebecca standing at check-in. "Hey, thanks for the book. I decided I like him after all." She smiled and nodded. "Yeah, well, I'm glad." He realized that he could fall in love with her; perhaps he already had.

They were on the same flights to Denver and O'Hare, but rows apart. He saw her one last time at baggage claim in Chicago, where she embraced a handsome Caucasian man. Two beautiful, caramel-colored children swarmed around their feet. This was her final surprise to him.

When he stepped out of the airport, he took a deep breath and tasted the familiar stench of jet fuel. He rode the shuttle to his Audi, switched on NPR, and drove home along familiar byways. He began to feel comfort from the familiarity around him. He pulled into the tree-shaded driveway, tooted the horn twice, and slipped out of the leather seat. He stood in the drive and looked at his beautiful home, surprised that it still meant something to him.

"Amanda!" he called in the entryway, where a chandelier hung and a curving stair ascended to the second floor. Her reply came from upstairs. "Honey, I'm doing my hair. Can you be ready by five? We're having dinner at the Rosenthal's ... Oh! and you've got messages." The hair dryer revved up to a whine.

Stan left his bag on the landing and entered the office with his briefcase. The answering machine blinked. He sat down with pad and pen and hit the playback button. The machine whirred. "Stan, Jerome. Welcome home. Listen, there's been a change in the Center Drug case..." He scribbled some notes, glancing occasionally at the framed family photograph on his desk, the one from Christmas in the Bahamas. In the picture, he looked young and confident. He wanted that confidence back.

While unpacking his briefcase, he found Mencius. He flipped it open to something he had read on the plane, but it somehow didn't have the same meaning now. From the leaves of the book fell the list of his vows, sliding beneath his chair. He scooped it up, studied it briefly with an odd feeling of embarrassment, and slipped it back into the book. He set

Mencius aside and looked around his office. He felt as if he had just awakened from a dream. He could hear Amanda coming down the stairs, and he quickly covered Mencius with that morning's *Wall Street Journal*. She flew into the office and hugged him. He was overwhelmed by her perfume. Her hair was a masterpiece from the pages of a fashion magazine.

"Honey, why didn't you call back about the plumber? I was in a panic. I didn't know what to do."

He saw her as if for the first time, her coiffed hair, painted lips, highlighted eyes.

"Well? Was it great? Are you glad you went?"

"I'll tell you on our way to Jack and Carol's. Where are the kids? I want to see them."

"They're at the park with Lupe. Can't it wait until morning?"

"Sure... I just thought..."

"Well, get going then," she shooed him off with a wave of her hands. "You always make us late!" Amanda rushed off, leaving Stan marooned in a time warp.

Stan pushed aside the *Journal* and picked up Mencius. He squeezed the book in his hands and held it as a tangible reminder of the world of ideas, a world in which he had lost himself for a while the way Alice lost herself down the rabbit hole. He slipped the book onto a shelf between a John Grisham novel and *Hot, Flat, and Crowded*, by Thomas Friedman. He checked his watch and slowly climbed the stairs. ☆

Chapter 7 | First Snow

THE FIRST SNOW OF WINTER draws across the valley in thin curtains draped over the mountains like one of Christo's designs. Each successive curtain adds to the shroud dimming the wan light of a November morning.

He stands at the sliding glass doors, a mug of coffee in his hand. He feels the cool weather through a tattered bathrobe, ragged socks, saggy long underwear. His gray hair sticks up like straw, his silver mustache droops over his lips. A sudden gust of wind drives the snow crosswise, battering the dingy glass, leaving white blotches that melt and trickle down in wobbling streams.

He turns away from the sliding doors, sets down the mug, and rummages through a cardboard liquor box that holds his music collection. He digs through it until he finds the right mood: Mozart's horn concertos. He loads a portable CD player and settles back on the sofa, the only piece of furniture left in the apartment, threadbare, worthless, destined for the dumpster. He sinks into the foam rubber, a fellow discard, equally worn. The couch is where he has been sleeping during these last days in Aspen.

The first movement of his favorite concerto engulfs him like it always does, soothing in its soulful resonance. The orchestra drowns out the patter of the snow against the glass, beyond which a wall of dark gray clouds has erased the mountains across the valley. Resting his head against the couch, he is soon caught up in the phrasings of the horn. He closes his eyes and drifts with its melodic, hypnotic beauty.

He remembers Jeff, grinning like a chimpanzee, his long, blond hair spreading from beneath a pointed Peruvian cap...Jeff, with the red backpack, the shovel handle sticking out the top...Jeff, in the faded blue anorak, the patched bib overalls, the duct-taped gloves. Jeff's smile is white against dark brown cheeks and red, peeling nose. The old man sighs as he assembles pixels of color and shape from the memory chip of his brain. Seeing Jeff gives him solace the way the music does. The old man is not alone for this first snow of winter, not with the good company of Mozart and Jeff.

They are standing at the top of the peak on a sunny spring morning where Jeff strips his climbing skins from his skis with short, hard pulls. The skins come loose with the sound of fabric tearing. Jeff carefully folds his skins together and stows them in his pack. He clamps his boots into telemark bindings and checks his avalanche transceiver for the high, pulsing beep. He sidles toward the edge and looks over the cornice at a twenty-foot drop to the slope below. From there the pitch falls away, steep at the top, rolling out gently at the bottom. There is a beautiful symmetry to the vast field of snow below him, and the old man savors every detail. What elation he had felt then.

He jerks awake and pushes himself off the couch with a grunt and shuffles to the glass doors. He presses his palms against the cold and holds them there as the first snow drifts down. He is mesmerized by the hypnotic patterns of cascading flakes, each with its own distinctions, yet blurred among the whole.

The old man returns to the couch and sinks back into the soft cushions. He picks up the cold coffee mug. The cream has congealed. He sets the mug on the floor and leans his head back, listening to the melody of the horn as it communes with the orchestra. He coaxes his mind to bring Laura into view; her freckled cheeks, her green eyes blazing from beneath a wave of sandy brown hair. It's all as clear as the picture of her that he has packed in a box somewhere, a box he may never open again. He can remember the way she walked, how she stood to about his shoulder, how he had caressed the soft skin of her beautiful young body. He wonders where Laura is now, how many children she has, maybe even grandkids. He wonders where a lot of people are, the friends he had known over the years, friends made easily with a smile and lost by simply forgetting. They're all old now, he muses. Would they even recognize him, a specter

from a time when they were young, a time they all thought could never end?

He runs his hands over his legs and feels them with his fingers. They were strong once, but crippled now by arthritis and tendonitis. His knees are bone-on-bone where the cartilage used to be. His hips are shot. He's been living in a dump that was a dump even back in the day: peeling paint, flaking linoleum, a drooping, water-marked ceiling. He realizes that he and this apartment are on parallel tracks: bright and shiny in the sixties, capable in the seventies, serviceable in the eighties, patched together in the nineties, falling apart in the new millennium. Now this building is scheduled for the wrecker, so what does that say about him?

Suddenly restless, he pries himself off the couch and stands again at the glass doors. The snow, the first snow of winter, drifts lazily by. The storm has come to stay with the deep gray palor of an organized cold front. He gazes at the helter-skelter of tumbling flakes and realizes what a thrill this day once held for him. The first snow! He reflects again on Jeff and how they shared the same excitement at the start of winter. The ski plans they made! The adventures they would share! What the hell happened to his best friend? How could they just let each other go?

Marriage and mortgage, that's how it was for Jeff. Christ! They were like brothers. Time changed everything, and there is no going back. A pang of loss knots up in his chest. His lower lip trembles. His eyes burn. A single tear rolls down his rutted, weathered cheek, matching the pattern of water marks on the glass doors. Friends like Jeff are supposed to be forever. The old man has learned that nothing is forever.

The French horn takes him back. The melody captures him and he sways gently to the sonorous melody. He gets lost again in the whirling flakes. His thoughts drift to the top of the peak, back to the day, a golden day that he selects from all the hundreds of golden days he and Jeff shared. This day is painted with bold strokes. Memory is a refuge as much as the apartment has been, as much as Aspen has been. The old man runs through the images as if viewing a slide show projected on the backs of his eyelids: mountains, snow, ski turns, smiles, cold beers, sunsets.

It was all so easy, so simple, so natural. You did what you loved, and you did it with reckless abandon. Wealth was not a fat bank account or a palace on Red Mountain. The riches of the world were there for the taking on every summit he ever climbed, with every glorious day spent living free in the mountains, in all the peak experiences that touched his soul. You pledged your time—and sometimes your life—to your friends. You followed the fall line and fell in love every day. Gravity was a gift, not the curse it is today. The old man feels an upwelling of emotion that chokes him with a sob. The snow is falling past his eyes. The horn is lulling him into romantic introspection. He sees it all like a beautiful documentary.

Jeff is eager. He pulls his goggles over his eyes, grips his poles, works the straps across his knuckles. He taps down his baskets into the snow. He takes a deep breath and leaps off the peak as if stepping off a high-dive. He disappears over the cornice and lands below with a soft whoosh. From the waist down he vanishes in a puff of snow, then he's moving fast, faster, flying. He finds his rhythm and plunges into his turns, a plume rising behind him.

The old man, his eyes closed tight, loses count of the turns as Jeff bounces on his supple legs, laying down a set of perfect tracks past the band of sun-baked red rock where the bighorn sheep winter. The old man's heart pounds, measuring Jeff's turns with Mozart's rhythm as the CD spins and the snow whirls beyond the glass doors.

Jeff executes a wide, arcing turn and comes to a stop where the basin opens into an alluvial run-out above the creek, where willow canes poke up through the snowpack. Jeff raises his arms and a distant whoop carries up the mountain slope. The whoop becomes louder and louder until the old man suddenly opens his eyes. A car alarm is beeping in the parking lot. He stares out to where snow collects on the roofs and bumpers of cars. The car alarm stops and the old man focuses again on the concerto. The sound of the French horn is full and round. He breathes slowly, meditatively. His eyes relax to a distant view through the snow, beyond the glass doors. He loses himself in the deep gray clouds.

Many years have passed since the old man looked down a mountain between a pair of ski tips, but what a glorious way it was to see the world. Vast and still, steep and uniform, each run was inviting. Gravity exerts a powerful force at 12,000 feet, and the powder snow begged for his tracks to complement Jeff's. How trustingly he had yielded to the pull. What a life he had led in the mountains. He could hardly believe it was him, the same man.

He looks around the apartment, jarred momentarily by its hollow emptiness, the boxes near the door. How many moves have there been? The dilapidated miner's shack in the West End, the riverside apartment on East Cooper, a sunny room at Highlands Villas, a drab, noisy dorm at the Inn at Aspen, a closet-like condo at Silver King, the slum at the Agate, and now a tear-down ruin of a lodge where he signed on as maintenance man, bunking in one of the garrets. So, this is it. This is how it ends for him in Aspen. He submits again to the gravitational pull of the couch.

The music rises, the mellow horn of Mozart, the way he first heard it with Laura. He had been uncomfortable then, feeling nervous and out of place in the music tent amid the Aspen culture crowd. He had watched Laura's eyes as they scanned the orchestra. She had pointed out the instruments and told him about the compositions. His first concert, the horn concerto, was unlike anything he'd ever experienced. The sound flowed around him, through him. It frightened him with its intensity. Laura had brought that beauty into his life, that gift. Summers were spent sitting with her on the lawn, under the aspens.

He sighs, filling his lungs, the old, leather bellows, creaky and brittle against his tight ribcage. In the silent pause between movements, he hears the first snow of winter beating on the window, the wind jangling the chimes on his deck. Everyone else had moved out since the eviction notice was posted. He had begged them to let him stay until the end, and now he is the only one in the building, a ghost in his haunt, caretaker of the doomed.

Then begins the second movement, Romance. Laura had to explain it to him how the movements worked, that you didn't applaud during the breaks between them. More than once she had to silence his callused laborer's hands as he began to clap. He scolded himself for being dull to culture, for having an undisciplined mind. After Laura was gone, he began to hear the music with his own sensitivities, his own interpretations. He had to feel his way through his emotions, discovering a depth that only Laura could lead him to, but that he had to plumb on his own.

The music draws him deeper inside with its hypnotic strains. He closes his eyes and he's back on top of the peak beneath the impossibly blue sky. Thank God he has these memories, which he tailors to soothe and comfort and distract. He alone edits his life stories.

Half drowsing through the middle of the second movement, the old man sits up abruptly, remembering something. He stands, struggling for balance, and walks deliberately to the packing boxes. He pulls them open, one at a time, until he finds a thick braid of yarn from which a cluster of plastic-coated ski passes is tied. Each pass translates into a measure of his life, the memoirs of a skier.

He sorts through the passes and studies the pictures, exploring the nuances of his aging, how young and tan had turned to old and gray. The final picture shows the baggy eyes, hooked nose, and white mustache, framed by the characteristic woolen cap. He counts them: thirty-eight. He smiles, for he knows he has received a great and wonderful gift. He takes the bundle of ski passes back to the couch. He sits down and spreads out the clutter of plastic and braided string on the worn cushion. He is deeply tired.

Something comes to mind. He leans over and paws through a pile of newspapers on the floor. He finds the issue he's been saving. He turns to the folded over page in the classifieds where the vintage VW bus is pictured. How great would that be, loading up his boxes and driving down the valley in a VW bus. He had arrived that way in Aspen four decades ago, and he could depart that way, with a life epoch sandwiched in-between. If only he had saved some money, then things would be good.

His first bus, with the holes in the floor panels and the broken heater, had rattled up the two-lane highway. He had craned his neck to look up at the mountain peaks, excited like a boy on summer vacation. On his first day in Aspen, he found a job making beds at the Mountain Chalet. That was the start of his Aspen resume: hotel maid to dishwasher to prep cook to waiter to laborer to carpenter to ski patrolman to snow shoveler to bus driver to lift-op to handyman. Now there is only Social Security, from which he draws a pittance.

Absentmindedly, he shuffles to the glass doors, humming along with the last of the second movement. The wind has died and the sky is filled with soft, ephemeral, fluttering snow. He studies the clouds. They are dark enough to absorb a man's life and bury it in deep drifts. He watches the flakes tumble past his window and realizes that time moves like those flakes: never stopping, always changing. As soon as you grasp the present moment, it is past.

The third movement, Rondo, kicks off robustly, feeding him with lyrical energy. He abandons the window and goes digging through the cluttered hallway, then through the dark closet. He can't remember where he put them, or whether he has thrown them out. He goes through all the boxes, but his ski boots are gone. Somebody might be using them as flower pots, relics filled with earth, nurturing root systems where his feet had once snuggly fit. Why does he want them? He hasn't worn ski boots in ten years. He wants to touch them, look at them. Perhaps they can take him back to other ridges, other ski runs, other friends. If he could slide his feet in they might guide him back to something meaningful. Perhaps those boots could take him to that wonderful, carefree place where his future once lay before him in perfect, intertwining ski tracks down a mountainside.

In one box, he finds his medications—the prescriptions he's been hoarding for years—pain killers, sleeping pills, antibiotics. He studies them and realizes their potency. Here is another ticket out, he realizes.

Could he do it? He fondles a prescription bottle full of Percoset. He drops the bottle into his shirt pocket, straightens up, and wonders what brought him into the hallway in the first place. He pats his pocket and feels an odd sense of security. Whatever happens, he's got a way to handle the pain.

He returns to the couch, eases in again to the tired, old cushions, leans back, closes his eyes. His grizzled chin, white with three days of whiskers, sags beneath the moist gap of his mouth. He ponders what's next. South. Like a migrating bird, he'll go to New Mexico, Arizona, Death Valley. He has heard of a place in Arizona for people like him who own no ground other than what lies beneath their feet, or beneath their wheels. Some own nothing more than the shadows they cast on the earth. He might find others like him with uprooted lives, geriatric gypsies looking for a place to park. He will call that number in the classifieds as soon as the concerto ends. He'll make an offer on that bus. But how much can he scrape together? He's too tired to think about it, and he lets the newspaper fall to the floor.

The third movement leaps into the rapturous, energizing finale. Something touches the old man with a spectral, shadowy hand. He is oppressed by an acute attack of anxiety. His breathing comes shallow and fast, his pulse booms in his ears. Panicky, he gets to his feet and goes to the window. The snow is falling straight down in big, feathery flakes. The first snow of winter has piled an inch on the porch rail and shows no sign of letting up. The sky is dull, the gray hue that describes the life of an old man who has lived beyond his friends, beyond his loves, a man caught in the amber of his own faded dream, a simple man who seeks solace in music, an imaginative man who plays back his memories to an audience of one, a lonely man who wonders what happened to the years.

The concerto ends and then comes silence, deep, penetrating, uneasy silence. He suddenly needs air. He pulls the sliding door open on squeaky tracks and feels a blast of cold. He steps out onto the snow-covered deck in his stocking feet. The snow crystals bombard his face, stick to his eyelashes. He looks up into the white, tumbling flakes, blinking into an infinite universe cascading toward him. Frightened by the vision, he closes his eyes against the chaos of the storm and lets the first snow of winter settle over him. ☆

Chapter 8 | Fireweed

"...and foreign policy analysts conclude that there is little chance of a peace settlement and that the war will escalate. The president has called for an increase in troop activity..."

THE CAR RADIO DIES with the last sputter of the engine. "Good riddance!"

"Good riddance to what?" she asks.

"Good riddance to syphilization."

"Syphilis what?" she asks, looking quizzical.

"Syphilization—the crazy fucking world we're about to leave behind."

"Are you all right?" She studies me briefly for clues.

"Just right," I smile. "How could anything be wrong on our first date?"

She shakes her head. "This isn't our first date. Don't you remember the physics lecture?"

"Ah, yes, black holes and dark matter... Okay, so maybe that wasn't such a good idea."

She gives me that look again. "Are you sure this is such a good idea?"

"Trust me."

"Why should I?"

"Men's intuition, my dear. Men's intuition."

She shakes her head, laughing. Her auburn hair sweeps across her face, wafting a light and pleasing fragrance of flowers. I suddenly know that this is exactly the right idea. What better place can a man and woman get to know each other than under a mountain sky?

We get out of the old VW and haul the packs out from the backseat. We are met with the chatter of bird song, the buzz of insects, the murmur of the creek, the sigh of a fresh, cool breeze. The trail beckons through the aspens and conifers, asters, and cow parsnips. Three revolutions of the earth and ten thousand footfalls should provide surcease. It's the walking, said Thoreau, that sets us on our chosen path, and our path leads into the wilderness.

We ready our packs, but I can't get the radio babble out of my head, the monotone banter of dispassionate foreign policy analysts and their studied conclusions about the efficient management of the goddamned war. My mind works it over with deep-seated anger. Damn the international community and its failed diplomacy! Damn the war mongers! Damn the weapons designers! Damn the defense contractors! the extremists! the fanatics! Damn the militant clerics! the divine edicts! the hypocrites! Damn humanity for its willingness to perpetrate the slaughters and suicides and ethnic cleansings and purges and inquisitions and final solutions. It's all cloaked in the same lie—civilization.

"Damn it all!" I mutter.

She looks at me quizzically, this time with concern. "What exactly is bothering you?"

"Oh, just a little pent up frustration about the state of the world."

"Well, I'm glad it's nothing serious, then."

"No, just man's inhumanity towards man."

"I hope you packed the Prozac."

"This is my Prozac—a long walk in the woods—with you."

"Give me a hand, will you?"

I lift her backpack, holding it above her shoulders while she adjusts the straps. "Thanks, I've got it."

She cinches the waist strap and starts up the trail, which climbs steeply among the white trunks of tall, straight aspen trees, then switchbacks through the dark shade of spruce and fir. The pack covers her like a shell. I can see only the tortoise-like backpack, her long, suntanned legs, her leather hiking boots. My quick summation is that she's fit enough for the trip, but I wonder more about after the trip. Where is this trail really leading?

I haul my pack to my hips with a grunt, slip my arms through the straps, and cinch the waist belt. Leaning forward, I lurch up the hill as if walking into a stiff gale, the straps weighing with every step. It's always like this at the start.

Soon the only sound is the rush of the creek where it tumbles through the lush ravine below the trail. Clouds move across the valley, covering and uncovering the sun in a slow rhythm of brilliant hot light and cool shade. Leaning under the weight of my pack, I study the trail for my next footfall and notice the details—a flake of gray shale embedded in red dirt, an eroded tree root twisting like a snake, a gray patch of powdery silt, a tiny rivulet trickling over a gravel bar, the sharp-toed print of a deer. Her pack bobs ahead through tall serviceberry bushes with their delicate, white blooms, across a scree slope where the Maroon rocks are splotched green with lichen, into a forest glade where the air smells piney and moist.

On the winding footpath, climbing through delicate ferns and clusters of fragrant purple lupine, the news analysts finally fade. My mind clears and my spirit lifts. This deep verdant valley is calm and sheltering, filled with a centering peace. If I fail to notice the things around me, if I allow my mind to wander beyond my senses, then that other world comes back, the one made by man. With it comes the enervating dread of that storm cloud of war that's hurling lethal thunderbolts upon ancient kingdoms and setting the very heavens ablaze. Apocalyptic visions are a strange contrast to this world, a bizarre human obsession for which nature is the antidote.

I should not have read the news magazine on the breakfast table. I should not have looked at the pictures of the mother and her child who lay together in a dusty street, as if napping, carelessly sprawled against a broken stone wall. The mother wore a peasant dress with a flower pattern. The child was in a tunic and pants with a ragged hem. Rubble was strewn about. The caption read simply, with grim finality—*Poison Gas*—a brutal homage to the innocents and the technology of killing.

A brilliant splash of hot, pink fireweed blooms tall and torch-like along the trail. I reach out and caress a bloom, causing the flowers to sway on their lithe, supple stems. The trail meanders through an aspen grove where the leaves rattle and twist in a light breeze. A ray of sun bursts from a puffy cumulus cloud and illuminates the deep green tundra on the steep ridge 3,000 feet above.

She stops and turns, waiting in a small meadow. Dozens of columbines thrust above a carpet of grasses and shrubs, their blue and white pedals dipping in the breeze. She smiles upon these flowers for having smiled upon her. The baseball cap she wears shields her face from the sun and casts a shadow line across her cheek. She looks tomboyish and cute.

"Everything good?" I ask.

"This is so beautiful."

Her smile is contagious. She loves this as much as I do.

"I'm glad."

"Is the Prozac working?" she asks.

"Just what the doctor ordered."

"Good."

She continues hiking up the trail. I watch her go, feeling a heightened sense of promise. It was only two weeks ago that we met at the post office. Our boxes are one row apart, so we traded smiles, said hello a few times, talked about skiing, the weather, current events in Aspen. When I finally summoned the courage to ask her out she laughed and said she was relieved. Now she didn't have to ask me.

I hear a droning buzz and I notice a bee making its rounds through the columbines, hovering from one flower to the next, taking nutrition in return for pollination in a symbiosis that ensures life for both bee and flower, the fertilizer and the fertilized. I look back up the trail and she has disappeared around a bend.

By late afternoon the sun drops behind the western ridge. Shadows grow and stretch across the valley. We make camp in a small meadow near the creek where moles have churned the soil into meandering hummocks of soft dirt. We compress the abandoned eskers, stomping with our boots to smooth out a tent site.

She walks off carrying a towel and a fresh shirt, pushing aside willows to reach the stream. I snap together aluminum poles, stretch the thin nylon tent over them, push metal stakes into the soft ground. I throw our sleeping bags into the tent, our downy bed. She returns with damp hair and a clean T-shirt. I have a pot of water on the camp stove for tea. It hisses quietly. A container full of my homemade elk stew is ready near the stove after the tea water boils.

"My turn," I tell her.

I find a place among the willows where the stream runs over flat, smooth rocks. I shed my clothes, drape them over willows, wade into the numbing cold stream and stand with aching bare feet in the rushing ice water that surges against my knees. Each splash of icy snowmelt brings an involuntary gasp. When I'm done washing, I rinse my shirt, wringing it until my hands ache with the cold.

Tea is steeping in our cups when I return. She has the stew sizzling in the pot. A few mosquitoes circle languidly in the cooling air. The shadow line of sunset is near the top of the ridge. The alpine tundra is lit with alpenglow. Cirrus clouds stretch across the sky, their undersides reflecting the rosy light. A faint, pink glow spreads over the valley as we break dark bread from a dense loaf and ladle the hot stew into our bowls. We eat with few words, then swab our bowls clean with the bread and rinse them in the creek. In the calm, quiet of dusk we stretch out on our sleeping pads and watch the stars appear.

"See the dipper?"

"Where?"

"The handle is touching the ridge."

"Now I see it."

"That's the North Star, near the top of that big spruce."

The cool of night settles on our camp and dampens everything with

dew. A narrow swath of stars and the blackness of deep space spans the void between the high ridges. The hoot-hoot of an owl rises faintly from down the valley. I draw my pad closer and snuggle into her. A bright planet shines overhead. I hold her in my arms, and we feel the welcome of each other's warmth against the glittering mysteries of the cosmos.

In the morning, the sun is slow to reach the valley floor, so we doze in the coolness. When the sun strikes the tent, the air becomes greenhouse hot. The sun glows through the yellow fabric and evaporates the dew drops on the rain fly. The creek makes a gentle purr. Birds flit in the brush and the air hums with insects.

"Top 'o the morning, dearie!"

"Top 'o the morning to you," she laughs.

I get the stove going and make coffee, strong and black. She fries eggs scrambled in a shaken jar. Packed up and ready to climb to the pass, we remove our watches and stash them deep in our packs. The sun is our clock.

The trail winds, twists, switchbacks, climbs. We cross boulder fields, splashing tributaries, avalanche zones choked with broken trees. Flowers are everywhere. We walk through a meadow where a pair of swallowtail butterflies cavort on warm air currents. The upper valley opens where the glaciers dished it out from solid rock that was once molten and flowing and rising under deep tectonic pressure. In the thin air near the pass, a saddle on the smooth ridgeline at the head of the basin, our pace is slow and plodding. We breathe hard, short-stepping up the final switchback through stunted Krummholz trees that cling tenaciously to life, their thick, sturdy trunks anchored in the rocky earth by roots that grip like clenched fingers.

From the pass, we gaze over a vast range of craggy peaks. Hungry, we break bread and open a can of sardines, eating them from our fingers, dripping with olive oil. Bright, diminutive alpine flowers carpet the tundra where the marks of sharp, cloven hooves evince mountain goats or bighorn sheep. Below us, the basin spreads out green and undulating, stepping down in small benches to the lake, a still, flat mirror reflecting clouds and the sturdy, protective ridges that wall in this magnificent refuge. We dangle sardines over each other's open mouths, the oil dripping on our chins. Our laughter is absorbed into space, diffused into the vast blue sky and the billowing clouds that float magnificently overhead.

A sudden, chill wind has us pulling sweaters and jackets from our packs. Steep switchbacks lead us down into the meadow, lush with flowers of every shade. We tiptoe through them to avoid trampling the delicate blossoms. We make camp on the tundra next to a huge boulder of Maroon sandstone. We stretch our legs and watch the clouds go by, their shadows racing across the basin.

A strange sound occasionally wafts up to us from the lower valley. Binoculars reveal a congealed mass of gray shapes a quarter mile below the lake. The sound of bleating sheep rises into the basin. We trade the glasses to watch them and the lone shepherd who tends them, regarding the shepherd as a kindred spirit, equally distanced as we are from the rest of the world.

"Maybe we could become shepherds and live here all summer. Could you do that?" I ask.

"I don't know about the sheep."

"Oh, that wouldn't be so baaa-d."

She nudges me with her elbow. "Very funny."

"Should I feel sheepish?"

"You!"

She wrestles me down and pins my wrists to the ground. Her eyes are bright. She suddenly leans down and kisses me. We entwine our arms and legs while rolling on the soft ground. Our hearts beat together. Our smells mingle.

Later, we hike up into the basin where a spring bubbles from a tuft of thick, green moss. Bog orchids bloom around a limpid pool at the edge of a boulder field. The water is icy cold and clear. We drink it from our cupped hands, then dip-fill two pans and return to camp, trying not to slosh the water. With the stove hissing, we sit cross-legged on our sleeping pads. Our eyes sweep the ridges encircling the basin. We examine the wildflowers at our feet.

The basin is a gentle place, and we ease into the deep quiet. Red wine from a plastic juice bottle goes well with spaghetti. After dinner we take a walk, holding hands. Each of us makes a silent pledge that will not be translated into words for many months. There is no need to articulate the impulses of our hearts. We are content to have our bond unspoken, not wanting to formalize the undefined, the wonderful. This wild place invites freedom from words, from definitions, from obligations.

The sheep quiet down at dusk. We are happy to share the basin with them and the shepherd. We see the flicker of his fire, but we don't return it. The stars are our fire. We huddle together in our own warmth. The flowers have closed their petals. The surface of the lake has turned flat and metallic. She leans her back against my chest and I fold my arms around her.

Later, we trade positions and I feel her warmth move into me. Her hands soothe my shoulders where the heavy frame pack gnawed. Muscles and skin respond to her touch, and I'm aware of a deeper feeling that her touch awakens. Our bed is soft that night on the spongy tundra that contours to tired hips and shoulders.

The morning dawns with gathering clouds, their undersides dark and glowering. Pancakes with maple syrup and sausage complement strong coffee with evaporated milk from a tin. We break down camp and hurriedly pack. Drizzle patters across the basin beneath a wisp of cloud that sweeps past. Behind it, to the west, dark clouds line up portentously, like a squadron of dirigibles.

"Wish we had another day," she muses.

"I wish we had a week, a month, a year."

A deep roll of thunder echoes across the basin. We sling on our packs and are soon panting up the switchbacks leading to the pass. The lake is slate gray and corrugated by wind. The shepherd's camp is deserted;

the sheep have moved down into the timber. A distinct black line marks the storm's leading edge, with drifts of rain trailing behind. The storm moves over the basin and crosses the lake.

At the pass, we drop packs and pull on rain jackets. She takes the lead on the descent into the narrow valley while I pause a moment to face what's moving in on the strengthening wind. There's excitement in the latent power and dark fury menacing overhead. I feel my mood shifting like the weather. I regret returning to that other world where my soul can become deadened with disquiet and sorrow. The echoes of that world seem to emanate from the deep reverberations of thunder rolling over me, rattling my rib cage. Lightning artillery begins shelling the ridges with fusillades of electricity.

I hurry after her as the storm breaks and we're hit by rounds of hail machine-gunned from a pitch black sky. The hail pings off our packs and stings our legs. A lightning flash arcs like a missile that crashes into the ridge just above us. Half a second later a sharp report splits the air. We make a dash for the sheltering trees, skip-jogging down the trail, ignoring the weight of our packs. The hail changes to rain and the rain turns heavy and drenching.

Heads down, rain running off the hoods of our jackets, we splash through forming puddles. The trail becomes a rivulet of rainwater where pellets of hail gather in the eddies, a white crest against the muddy flow. Salvos of lightning strike the ridges on both sides. Concurrent flashes create a strobe effect. The thunder is continuous, a deep, sonorous booming. The air smells of rain-washed mountains, a bouquet of spruce pitch blended with grasses, sedges, flowers, the redolence of the earth itself. There is no sweeter smell.

I no longer hear her footsteps, so I stop and turn. She is a dozen yards behind, walking placidly down the trail in her wet and shining blue jacket, the hood shrouding her face. On one side of the trail is a yellow-green willow thicket, the leaves glimmering with raindrops. On the other is a spray of neon pink fireweed standing head-high and nodding under the rainfall. The ridges are misty with torn clouds ripped from the dark storm.

She looks up and smiles, and I am suddenly taken by how lovely she is in the pouring rain, how beautiful among the bright flowers. There are droplets of water on her cheeks and a sparkling light in her eyes. Perhaps we are seeing each other for the first time under this cloud of storm and fire. Here is our moment, a place in time that is just for us, just for now. There is no reason to rush back to the known world, so we stand in the rain and let it wash over us. ☆

Chapter 9 | The Third Body

THE POLICE SCANNER PULSES AN ALARM IN THE NIGHT: "...avalanche deaths ...Pearl Basin ...two bodies recovered ...third body remains buried ...rescue resumes in the morning."

In the predawn darkness a team gathers at Mountain Rescue headquarters on deserted Main Street. Rescuers gulp coffee, scarf down sweet rolls, assemble gear. A Denver TV news crew sets up a transmitting truck on the street. A satellite dish angles skyward.

Charlie Butler, the sole survivor, is affixed with a microphone and told where to stand. He squints into the lights and describes how the snow fractured between his skis, how he watched his friends disappear. Charlie vows to help with the search. His young but haggard face will appear on the Morning News.

The sky is dark when the convoy of rescue vehicles sets off against a blustery wind that shakes snow loose from the boughs of evergreens. Wind-driven snow filters through headlights that sweep across tight curves as the road twists and turns, climbing above a deep river gorge. The road ends at a huge embankment of snow piled high by the plow truck. The sky brightens. Packs and rescue equipment are strewn across the staging area. Charlie shadows the rescue leader, the man whose helmet has SAFETY stenciled on the back.

The leader turns on him. "Look, Charlie, we really don't need you on this."

"They're my friends," pleads Charlie. "I'm the only one who can find her. I'm going if I have to ski all the way in myself."

"Okay! It's your party," quips the rescue leader, "but you stick with me. Understand?"

Charlie nods and gathers his pack, skis and poles.

A fleet of snowmobiles is loaded with gear. Probe poles are strapped to their sides. Engines whine. The air reeks of exhaust. The sleds roar off, some towing gear-laden ski trailers, others with ropes towing rescuers on skis, their faces covered with masks and goggles against the bitter January cold. Charlie slings on his pack, just as he did twenty-four hours earlier. A pink blush of sunrise spreads over white summits. There is raw, rugged beauty here, but Charlie doesn't see it anymore. Perhaps he never will again.

Charlie straddles the seat behind the leader and they bump and jolt up the track. Charlie gazes dispassionately at the mountains rising up on all sides. The machines growl up the track through dark timber, past stands of aspen, across open snowfields. The cold numbs Charlie's cheeks and nose. When the sun breaks over the eastern ridge, its rays are diffused by cirrus clouds blown in tatters by the jet stream.

Charlie thinks of his friends. It seems impossible that so much could happen in such a short time. He pictures them on the trail as they were only yesterday: Stinson's beard frosted white; Roger's peaked hat with the tassel waving; Mira gliding along, her squeaking binding keeping rhythm. His mind replays the events. Charlie doesn't want it to, but he's unable to shut it off, and the picture congeals.

It starts with a beautiful day, clear and sunny and full of expectations. They are in high spirits, laughing and joking, psyched for an adventure in the snow. It's what they live for: a day in paradise with great friends, a soulful connection with nature, the ever alluring mountains. The memory suddenly snaps into terrible focus. Charlie is almost at the top of the basin, tirelessly breaking trail. The others are not far below. He kicks his ski for the final switchback to the top of the ridge. Something cracks, everything shatters. It all comes apart, tumbling down around him. Charlie is knocked down, rolled over, and spit out. He struggles to stand, gasping for breath, his heart racing. Above him, the fracture line is a ragged cliff eight feet high, fifty yards across. Below him is a sea of snow blocks from the broken slab. His friends have vanished.

Charlie frantically scans the debris. There is something on the snow below and to the right. He quickly clicks out of his bindings and crashes through an obstacle course of snow blocks. He finds Stinson's pack. He flings off his own pack, unstraps his shovel, and begins digging. A foot down he hits a ski tip. He follows the ski to a boot, follows the boot to a leg that is violently twisted. He finally uncovers Stinson's face and finds a death mask. Charlie jerks him out of the hole and lays him out in the snow. He tries mouth-to-mouth. He slaps Stinson, shouts at him, screams at him. He pumps Stinson's chest. Nothing. He curses and screams, then switches off Stinson's beacon and studies his own. The indicator arrow points southwest.

Minutes later he finds a glint of neon yellow: Roger's ski pole. He digs frantically and finds Roger four feet under, face down. Roger's skis are wedged in by snow blocks. One of his arms is twisted under, the wrist still looped into a ski pole. It takes eight deadly minutes to get Roger out. Charlie tries to breathe life into Roger, forcing air into his lungs. His chest inflates and falls, again and again, but there is no pulse. After five minutes, Charlie collapses in exhaustion. "My fucking God!"

Charlie switches off Roger's beacon and searches methodically, praying for a signal. His heart is in his throat. Mira must have forgotten to turn on her beacon. Charlie climbs atop a block of snow and studies the trajectory of the slide, guessing where Mira might be. There is no sign of her. Charlie sits on a snow block and hears the wind. It is the loneliest sound he has ever heard. A deep shiver takes hold and rattles his core. His bones are ice. His blood is slush. His hands are numb. He is freezing. Charlie Butler skis for help through a vague, foggy nightmare. He telephones from the Pine Creek Cookhouse. The first rescuers arrive that evening. They find Stinson and Roger the way Charlie had left them. They search until dark for Mira.

The night passes endlessly for Charlie, and now he is retracing his steps. The rescue leader's sled roars up the trail and Charlie bounces and sways with the machine. Today they'll find Mira, beautiful, petite Mira. How characteristic that the last one found is Mira, always last, always struggling to keep the pace, plodding relentlessly at the rear. Patient

Mira, just happy to be there, telling them not to wait, always smiling. She must be patient now, one last time. They are coming for her.

A deep dread runs through Charlie as the snowmobiles draw closer to the basin. The trail crosses one avalanche chute after another. Rescuers cross at intervals, revving their machines past the run-out zones where trees lie tossed and broken. They cross the creek on a snow bridge, just below the basin. Rescuers are gathered there and the leader shuts off his machine.

Charlie peers around the leader's shoulder. There are two body bags on the snow cinched tight with straps. Charlie jumps off the machine and shoves his way through the rescuers. He drops to his knees and touches one of the cold, hard bundles. Tears drip onto the black plastic. Strong hands suddenly grip Charlie and pull him off. The leader and a man wearing a ski mask drag him away. The other rescuers turn their faces.

"Get a hold of yourself, damnit!" whispers the leader. "It makes it harder, don't you get that?" Charlie feels gut shot. He stares at the black bags on the white snow.

"Okay, guys, we ski from here," shouts the leader. "Follow the flags. We need probes, so take a bundle."

Charlie Butler stretches climbing skins onto his skis. He glances up at the high ridge where the slide broke. He recalls that it was here, in the lower basin, where Stinson had suggested a gradual traverse. Charlie had other ideas. He led off without a word, intending to take the ridge head-on. They had all followed, as trusting friends do.

Charlie looks up at the ridge. The fracture line is etched just below the crest, a jagged scar. There are rescuers plodding up ahead and others still arriving on sleds. Some strap on snowshoes and leash rescue dogs. The trail into the basin is marked by small, orange flags that flutter and pop in the rising wind. The rescuers march in a slow, plodding line. Charlie takes a handful of probe poles and follows.

He notices a change in the weather. The cirrus clouds have congealed into a thick overcast. The wind screams as they reach timberline. Charlie follows the beaten track across the wind-scoured basin. Gusts of wind buffet him, so Charlie pulls his hood up over his head and tugs the closure strings. The rescuers before him plod slowly, enveloped occasionally by blasts of snow.

Charlie is suddenly hit hard by the altitude, by a lack of sleep, by the cumulative shock and fatigue of the last twenty-four hours. His legs turn lethargic and leaden. His lungs burn for oxygen. His heart thumps in his chest. The wind pushes against him and he staggers against each shuddering gust. His ski tip submarines beneath a layer of windblown crust, causing him to stagger and nearly fall. It takes him half a minute to recover his wind. He leans against his poles, hanging his head. Only Mira drives him on, waiting for him in the slide zone.

Ahead of Charlie, one of the rescuers sets his pack on the snow, pulls out a jacket, and struggles into it. A shrieking gust sweeps down from the ridge, lifts the pack into the air, and carries it out across the basin where it disappears in the gathering murk. The rescuer charges after it with a curse. Charlie sets his shoulder into each gust as they shove hard against him. The wind hits his legs, tugs on his pants, blasts his face with ice flecks. Charlie hears a strange, unearthly sound. He takes a moment to identify it as the steady roar of the wind, a groaning, haunting wail coming from the ridge.

Charlie follows the fluttering orange flags to the avalanche site. Two groups of rescuers are probing in parallel lines. Charlie drops his probe poles and clicks out of his bindings. He looks back and sees the leader coming up behind him.

"They should be higher," shouts Charlie, cupping his voice against the wind, pointing toward the ridge.

"We'll get there," shouts the leader.

"No. They've got to go higher!" insists Charlie.

"You're not calling the shots. Take a probe and join a line."

Charlie knows where Mira disappeared. He takes a probe pole and struggles upward through the snow blocks. He moves past the probe lines and works his way up toward the ridge. A hand is suddenly on his shoulder. Charlie is pulled roughly back.

"Nobody goes up until I say so," shouts the leader, gasping for air from the effort to catch him. "Join a probe line or I'm sending you down."

Charlie stumbles back to where the probe lines are working, rescuers moving together, shoulder-to-shoulder. Charlie joins a line. "Forward... probe!" shouts the leader. "Forward...probe!"

Charlie advances in unison with the others. On command, he punches his long, thin probe into the snowpack. The snow is dense and the pole penetrates only three feet. Charlie raises and pushes again. He gains another two feet. He pushes again and again. It takes him five thrusts before the probe is up to the hilt, fifteen feet, and still no bottom. Charlie realizes the futility of the search, realizes how huge is the volume of snow. Mira is buried somewhere underneath it all.

One of the probers meets resistance eight feet under. The probe leader tests the pole. He cannot push it further. He withdraws the pole and plants a small orange flag. He signals the shovelers. The probe line moves on. Two men follow behind with shovels and begin burrowing beneath the flag. More rescuers arrive. Soon there are three probe teams working. Behind each of them are half a dozen search pits. The pits are deep and dark except for the rim that glows cold blue. Two avalanche dogs—a golden lab and a shepherd—prance around each new pit, tails wagging as their trainers set them to their task.

A screaming roar comes down from the ridge. It sounds like a jet plane. Charlie crouches on one knee and meets the gust with his shoulder. The man on the probe line next to him is blown down. The entire probe line topples with him. Charlie feels the wind is trying to push them out of the basin, trying to keep Mira a prisoner in the snow. The probe line reassembles and continues its slow march across the slide zone. Forward...probe! Forward...probe! It's an exhaustive, repetitive routine. Plunging the pole quickens Charlie's breathing, tires his hands and arms. Forward...probe! Charlie advances two paces and plunges his pole.

The wind roaring over the ridge adds to the cacophony of yelping avalanche dogs, shouting probe leaders, and the stereophonic squawking of radios. Charlie is suddenly overwhelmed by an unbearable multitude of screams that echo in his head. A few yards away is an empty pit. Forward...probe! Charlie drops his probe pole and lurches for the blue hole. At its mouth he drops to his knees, staring into the tunnel, which angles downward into the darkness. Charlie slides down the tunnel head first and lands in a small chamber. All is silent under the snow. Charlie has found a den, a safe haven from the wind. He curls himself into a ball, hugging his knees to his chest, trying to soothe the demons that scream in his skull. Tears flood his eyes. He's wracked by convulsive sobs.

The tunnel darkens as someone crawls in behind him. A headlamp shines in his face. "Charlie! Let's go!" Charlie doesn't budge. He wants to stay in the comfort of the snow. He needs the silence, the same silence that enshrouds Mira. He feels closest to her here.

The leader lunges forward. He takes Charlie by the hood of his jacket and pulls. Charlie bats away the hand and scuttles deeper into the chamber. Charlie is left in the muted silence. Soon the tunnel darkens again. The leader's headlamp shines into Charlie's stricken face. Another man is there, the one wearing the face mask. The leader slides down into the chamber. He kneels, looking at Charlie. "It's over!" he says.

"You found her?"

"No. We're going down."

"Not without Mira. You said you'd find her."

"I said, we're out of here."

Charlie balls himself up, wraps his arms around his head, pulls his knees up to his chest. The leader grabs Charlie firmly by the back of his jacket. The man with the face mask reaches in and together they wrestle Charlie out of the tunnel. When they emerge, with Charlie in tow, they are bathed in a strange light.

The wind has abated and the overcast has thinned. Filtered rays of sunlight pierce the haze in brilliant shafts that set the airborne snow glistening. With the sun there is light and shadow, a contrast that sharpens the features of the landscape. The ridges loom with foreboding rock and ice. The chunks of avalanche debris look like quarried marble, jagged and sharp, with precise edges. Probers raise their eyes. Shovelers emerge from pits into an ephemeral light.

The leader grips Charlie by the shoulder. "I want you off this mountain! Bart, watch him." The man in the face mask stands over Charlie.

The light changes. The sky dims. Clouds sweep back across the wan sun. The wind rears up. A wall of cloud appears over the ridge, gray, the color of snow. Bart motions to Charlie. "Let's go!" Charlie wonders where Mira could be, why the snow is holding her. What more can it want? What more can she give?

Charlie is suddenly numb. He stumbles disconsolately through the snow blocks. He finds his skis and mechanically strips off his skins. Bart shadows him. Charlie fastens his bindings and picks up his poles. He pushes off on the drifted track. The surface is hard crust with pockets of fluff. Skiing is impossible. Charlie falls, picks himself up, struggles in an awkward snowplow down toward tree-line, away from the banshee cry of the wind. When he reaches the snowmobiles at tree-line, Charlie notices that the body bags are gone. Energy bars and hot coffee are dispensed from a snowmobile trailer. A woman in a rescue jacket hands Charlie a cup poured from a steaming thermos. Charlie sips the coffee and returns the cup to the woman. She recognizes him and nods her head with a knowing glance.

Charlie Butler begins the long descent down the narrow, twisting road. He ignores the snowmobiles as they pass. He ignores the leader, who offers him a ride. He ignores the wind and the burning cold on his face. He feels nothing, aware only of a deep-seated numbness that may never go away. He is oblivious to the first flakes of snow as they tumble from the darkening sky.

Dusk surrounds him. He skis the trail alone, working over the regrets that will take the rest of his life to sort through. Behind him the storm howls and batters the basin where Mira is deaf to it all. Charlie feels the push of the wind as it shoves against his back. Along the road on the valley floor the top strand of a barbed wire fence vibrates in a high, wailing cry.

*   *   *

There is heat in the early July sun as Charlie hikes up to the basin. He favors a tent site on a plot of soft tundra sheltered by granite boulders. He drops his pack and peels off his sweaty shirt, digs out a dry one and slips it on. He pulls his shovel from his pack and climbs to the top of the shrinking snowfield. He unzips binoculars from their case and scans the surface. Something dark protrudes from the snow.

Charlie scrambles up to the place. He drops to his knees and touches a glove. Inside it he feels Mira's hand. He begins to dig, carefully scraping away the snow. He reaches a layer of ice and sets aside the shovel. He brushes the ice clean with his glove. Through the crystalline opaqueness he sees her face. Mira lies embryonic within the ice bubble that formed in the last of her warmth.

Charlie climbs slowly down from the snowfield. He shudders in a cool breeze, sitting back against a sun-warmed boulder. A thin rivulet of snowmelt trickles through the tundra. A cluster of columbines gently waves. Charlie Butler watches the flowers nod and bend. He hears the soft gurgle of water. He feels the welcome warmth of the sun. ☆

Chapter 10 | The Big Hill

THE SUN CRESTS THE HIGH PEAKS of the Sawatch Range, glinting through tall, conical spruce and fir. Black and white nuthatches flit among the straight, white trunks of aspens as dawn streaks across the snow-patched basins above the wide valley of the Taylor River.

Kate is the first to see the man as she lifts a pail of water from the creek. He approaches on horseback, leading a pack animal. She stays low and watches him ride through the silvery, dew-tipped willows. She leaves her pail and reports to Dave Wilson, who is examining the axles on a matched pair of heavy freight wagons.

"There's a man comin', Dave," she says with a note of alarm, her pulse racing with excitement. She points toward the willows along the creek bed.

Wilson jumps onto the wagon and pulls a rifle from its place beside the seat. He looks across the willows and sees the man astride his horse. Kate watches from behind the wagon.

The man wears a worn woolen military-style jacket and a wide-brimmed hat. His ragged canvas pants are crudely patched and covered to the knees with leather leggings. He wears calf-high moccasins laced with leather thongs. A thick beard obscures his features and long, dark hair cascades to his shoulders. He rides a big chestnut mare and leads a packhorse loaded with canvas panniers. A rifle butt protrudes from a scabbard on the man's saddle. A long knife in a beaded leather sheath dangles from his belt. He pivots his mount around a willow and faces Wilson's rifle.

"Seen your fire," says the man.

Wilson studies him from the wagon, his rifle at the ready. He sums him up instantly, as is his nature with men. "Like some breakfast?"

The man nods. "Sure would."

The man sits Indian-style on the ground near the smoking fire. Over biscuits, bacon, and hot coffee, he describes the buzz of activity in the mining camps he's seen in the Gunnison Country, from Irwin to Gothic. "Can't find a piece of ground that aint already been spoke for. Folks covering them hills like ants." Wilson and his party listen intently. "Where you folks headed?"

Wilson doesn't answer. Instead, he describes their travels during a month-long odyssey from Black Hawk through South Park, Fairplay, Alma, over Mosquito Pass to Leadville, down the Arkansas to Buena Vista, over Cottonwood Pass and now here, to the headwaters of the Taylor. Wilson says nothing of the big hill ahead or of their intentions for the Roaring Fork. The man listens attentively, forking the last morsels off his tin plate.

Wilson looks the man over carefully. He assumes they're about the same age, late 20s. The man has ravenously eaten a mountain of food, a lone wolf on the move. Wilson decides this might be a good man to help get them over the big hill. His appetite indicates the likelihood of a willing hand. "Name's Wilson," he says, extending his hand. "Yours?"

The man gets to his feet in a smooth, sinuous motion. "Baker," he says, reaching out and taking Wilson's hand. "Dan Baker."

The old man standing next to Wilson, his chin sporting a thin swath of trimmed white beard, has been biding his time. He approaches and shakes Baker's hand, feeling a knotty strength, the palms callused and rough. He appraises the unflinching look in the man's light gray eyes and likes what he sees. "Name's Crandall, but they call me Grandpap, cause I'm older'n most men in this here country." He gestures to a stout, middle-aged woman standing with a girl near the wagons. "This here's my wife, Margaret, and our daughter, Kate."

"Pleased," says Baker with a nod. He judges Grandpap to be in his late fifties, married to a woman many years younger.

Fremont, the muleskinner, keeps his distance, feeling there's no sense in rushing things. He studies the man carefully, noting every detail. The moccasins are elk or deer hide, the jacket crudely tailored from an old cavalry coat, the beaded knife sheath Indian-made, probably Sioux.

"Henry," says Wilson, turning toward Grandpap, "can you and me have a few words?" The old man nods and moves away from the fire. "Excuse us, Baker," says Wilson, and follows Grandpap past the wagons to where the teams are tethered. Baker glances at 18-year-old Kate, who stands by the wagon near her mother. The women's eyes are fixated on him. "Mighty tasty grub, ma'am," he smiles through his beard. Kate smiles and Margaret notices a blush on her daughter's cheeks. Baker sees it, too. "Kate. Take the man's plate." Kate does as she's told, a shy smile on her face.

Wilson and Grandpap move off and put their heads together. Grandpap nods and the men return. "We could use another hand with these wagons, Baker," says Wilson. "You might consider crossing the range with us and having a look at the new country."

"You goin' over?" he asks, nodding toward the ridge above.

"Yep," says Grandpap, "Lord willin'."

"Anybody else been over? They got a road in?"

"We seen two sets of wagon tracks goin' up—none comin' down."

"How much you payin'?" asks Baker.

"Half a dollar a day, grub included."

Baker shakes his head slowly. "That aint much of a wage."

"You ever work mule teams?" asks Grandpap.

Baker nods. "Plenty. I was a teamster for the UP in Laramie three years runnin'."

"Railroad man, eh?" affirms Grandpap. "Well, I s'pose we can pay a dollar a day...and a five-dollar bonus if you stick with us 'til we get down on the other side."

Baker scratches his neck, thinking.

"It'll be worth your while, Baker," encourages Wilson. "We need a good hand, and there's opportunity for a fella over that hill. Least, that's what they tell us."

"I hear tell there's opportunity over every hill," says Baker, "and I crossed enough to know it aint always so."

He surveys the faces in the circle around him. Wilson is sincere, honest. The old man and his wife have grit. The grizzled man with the flinty eyes wearing a Confederate cap and three days of whiskers is a hard-bitten muleskinner, no doubt about it. The girl is pretty; all young girls are pretty. He likes the feel of this party. The grub is good and a dollar a day is more than he's making now. Still, a doubt haunts him. Tying up with a party of emigrants requires something of a man that doesn't always fit with his way of being. Social graces are called for, and then there's the bother of doing things the way somebody else likes them. He prefers being his own boss, living on his own terms, but there is something he needs from these people, something more than food and pay, something human to make up for three months of lone wandering.

"Alright," says Baker. "You got yourself a hand."

The old man pumps Baker's hand exuberantly. "You fell in with the right outfit, son."

By mid-morning, the wagons are loaded and the teams harnessed. The party sets out amid the shouting of men, the clanking of hardware, the creaking of wagons, the clatter of hooves on river rock. They tackle the first pitch through rock-strewn aspen groves. The track ahead is barely discernible. Wilson has scouted, so he takes the lead in his wagon.

The rough double-track merges with a rushing creek gushing through a narrow slot between rock outcrops. There is no other way through than to run the wagons up the middle of the creek bed. Wilson drives the lead wagon, with Grandpap sitting next to him. The water is up to the hubs as it churns through the notch. Fremont, the old muleskinner, handles the reins of the second wagon, with Margaret and Kate holding tight beside him. Dan Baker rides his chestnut. His packhorse and an extra saddle horse, belonging to Wilson, trail behind the last wagon on short leads.

After passing through the creek bed, Wilson stops the wagons to let the mules blow. From here the trail climbs steeply through scattered evergreens, willow thickets, and verdant glades sporting clumps of color-ful flowers. Burbling rivulets of snowmelt run in braided cascades down through it all. Wilson waves for Baker to come up.

"Go on up ahead, there, Baker. The trail may backtrack once or twice, and I want to make sure we're not doubling our efforts."

Baker nods and follows faint wagon tracks on a contour around the hill and up onto a grassy meadow where the previous party left a fire ring and beaten ground. From there the tracks veer up several steep pitches through sparse timber and huge, lichen-covered boulders. As he's work-ing his horse through a stand of spruce, a sage hen bursts from a shrub and beats loudly into the air. The chestnut shies and hops like a rabbit. Baker settles his horse and watches the bird glide into the timber. He nudges the chestnut on until they reach a hilltop where the timber ends and a large, grassy basin opens onto a deep blue lake. He sees where the trail traverses to a high ridgeline where a cornice of brilliant white snow snakes along like icing on a cake. He dismounts for a drink from the lake, lets his horse nibble the short grasses around the shore, then retraces his route to guide the wagons.

The wagons are too heavy to make the steep grades, so the mules are joined into a single team of four. They make two trips, one for each wag-on. This takes them into the evening, and Wilson judges that the animals are about spent for the day. They camp at the lake on green tundra dot-ted with yellow, pink and white flowers, the ground furrowed by gophers. The lake shimmers in a light, cool breeze that's welcome after a hot day. Fish hit the surface, leaving expanding ripples. At dark, a smear of stars brightens the night sky.

The party is exhausted and there is little talk around the campfire. After a dinner of salt pork and biscuits, Baker finds shelter in a stand of stunted spruce where he stretches out on a fragrant bed of cone scales. He wraps himself in a double layer of his wool blanket. The others bed down near the campfire. Aside from the shifting of the mules and horses, the night is still, with only an occasional breeze.

Wilson rouses them for an early breakfast. By mid-morning, under four horses, the wagons are brought, one at a time, up to a bench just beneath the ridge. On closer inspection, the snow on the ridge forms a twelve-foot cornice of icy wind-pack that curls over them in a frozen wave. They follow the wagon tracks, leading them to a steep cut in the cornice that has iced over. Wilson jumps down from the wagon and attempts to climb through the notch. He promptly slips and falls, sliding down on his backside. He picks himself up with a laugh.

"We either wait for that ice to melt, or we dig our way through," says Wilson. "I'm not much inclined to wait, so we best set ourselves to it."

Wilson pulls a double-headed pick and a steel-bladed shovel from his wagon. He begins hacking at the ice with the pick, producing a shower of ice crystals. Baker and Grandpap hike up and join the effort after procuring another shovel and a long iron pry bar. They take turns hacking away at the snow and ice while the sun slowly softens it.

As they bend their backs against the ice, Fremont unhitches the mules and leads them in their harnesses to a shallow tarn where they drink and snatch mouthfuls of tall grass. Kate and her mother make sandwiches with thick, dark bread, salt pork and slabs of yellow cheese. Kate hums a melody in a high, clear soprano that floats across the basin.

Each swing of Wilson's pick produces a shower of ice chips that glimmer in the sun. The men take turns pecking away at the hardened snow, panting with exertion in the thin air. Baker swings the pick a dozen times before his lungs heave. His breathing comes short and fast, and sweat glistens on his face. He pulls off his shirt in the cool air and hot sun. Progress is slow until Grandpap suddenly gets an idea. He hurries back to the wagons and rummages through a wooden crate. He returns with a stick of giant powder.

"Boys, you can lay off those shovels," he announces, brandishing the dynamite. "Wilson, see if you can bust a hole down into that ice with that bar. Could save us half a day."

Wilson takes the iron bar and scrambles up onto the thickest part of the hard pack. He plants his feet and raises and drops the bar, its point penetrating, deeper and deeper, until it punches through the ice and strikes solid ground. Wilson passes the iron bar down to Baker, who carefully passes up the dynamite, to which Grandpap has attached a long fuse. Grandpap passes up a box of matches.

"Better clear out," says Wilson. "Baker, help Fremont steady the teams. Grandpap, you best tell the women to duck under one of the wagons."

Grandpap and Baker sidestep down the ice-strewn slope. Grandpap stands behind the lead wagon with Kate and Margaret. Baker jogs to the tarn. Fremont takes hold of the mules, and Baker grips the bridles of the horses.

"Whenever you're ready!" shouts Grandpap.

Wilson strikes a match and sets it to the fuse, which sputters and hisses. Sparks shoot out as the flame races toward the hole in the ice. Wilson slips and slides down the icy track and runs for all he's worth across the lumpy tundra. He stumbles, nearly falls, but recovers. The others cheer him on. Laughing and out of breath, he sprints behind the wagon, whirls, and looks back at the ridge.

The blast rents the thin air with a crash. The cornice erupts in a geyser of ice and snow that sends shards of ice as far as the wagons. The animals shy, but Freemont and Baker hold them. Cheers go up. The cornice is blown wide open and the men soon have the route cleared to the ground. They drive the first wagon through the gap, then lead the teams down for the second wagon. Margaret and Kate are waiting on a grassy hummock by the tarn. Kate wears a necklace of bright blue flowers she has twisted together. Her face is brown from the sun and lightly freckled.

At the top of the ridge they rejoin the old wagon tracks, marked deeply in the soft tundra. Wilson tells them to break for lunch, and Margaret hands each of them a sandwich. The men stand at the edge of the ridge, gazing into the new country to the north where the mountain peaks are tall and ragged and white with snow. A plunging valley drops off below them. They can hear the distant rush of a creek.

Wilson can feel his heart beating with excitement for what this country promises. Grandpap looks across the mountains and assumes this is the place where he'll last out his days. Fremont considers the seeming impossibility of getting the mules and wagons and gear down in one piece. Baker wonders how many ridges and valleys are still untouched for a man like him to explore.

"Henry! Henry!" calls Margaret from the south side of the ridge. The men hurry over to where she stands with Kate, surveying the expanse of the Gunnison Country they are leaving behind. "We're not the only ones," she says, pointing into the valley. Far below, where the Taylor River snakes through a meandering swath of willows, the wagon road is faintly seen as a wavering thread. Tawny puffs of dust rise at regular intervals marking wagons and teams. The men squint against the sun.

"I'll be damned," says Wilson. "Guess others have been steered this way, too."

"They'll be followin' our tracks," says Grandpap. "Best get the jump on 'em. C'mon, folks, let's move!"

Wilson and Grandpap hustle back toward the wagons while Baker and Fremont stand transfixed by the migration in the valley below. The longer Baker looks, the more wagons he sees, some on the road from St. Elmo and Tin Cup, others in camps near the river, but all with the same thing in mind, the next big hill, the next new country.

Fremont shoots a stream of tobacco juice from his pursed lips and it smacks against a flat rock. "Never thought I'd see the day," the old man grumbles. "Whole blame country's on the move, and all headin' this way." Baker feels a new urgency to his life and a new promise for the country. He realizes that open land and a strong promise for the future is a draw that men will always follow. Like ants to a picnic, they will come. Fremont spits again, then nudges a big, loose rock down the slope with the toe of his boot. They watch the rock tumble and bounce. It picks up speed, careens off a boulder, launches into the air, and bounds over a ledge and out of sight. They hear it crashing through the timber below. "Best get a'goin' if we're gonna stay ahead of that crowd," growls the muleskinner.

"Only way to stay ahead of 'em is if you never stop movin'," offers Baker. The old man shakes his head, turns and sidles toward the wagons. Baker studies the valley a moment longer, then feels someone standing at his side. It's the girl, Kate. She studies the valley with him. He feels her presence, smells her sweetness, hears her soft sigh.

"Daugh-ter!" calls Margaret. Kate glances up at Baker. "Oh!" she says, then turns with a rustle of skirts and scampers toward the wagons. Baker turns and notices that Margaret and Wilson are watching him. "Baker! Let's move 'em up the ridge!" calls Wilson.

Following the wagon tracks is easier now because the tundra is soft and boggy. The wheel ruts are deep. The ridge undulates, so the mules must strain to pull their loads up, then strain against them going down. Afternoon storm clouds move in, low and dark, forcing them to shelter in a hollow hemmed in by stunted trees forming thick hedgerows. Thunder booms and rain beats down. At dusk, the downpour turns to drizzle, and they try in vain to light a fire. At dark, they settle for cold biscuits and jerked beef under a hastily rigged canvas. Baker notices Kate's eyes on him and that they veer off whenever he looks her way. Wilson seems to notice, too. The air is cold that night and damp from the rain.

The next day dawns clear and cold. They push off under a warming sun. The old tracks lead to a steep drop into the head of a drainage. They ease the wagons down to a swale where the ground is soft and the wheels sink into the earth. The second wagon, with Grandpap driving and the two women riding, gets bogged down axle-deep. Under Grandpap's whip, the animals thrash against the immoveable wagon and are soon up to their withers in muck. Fremont and Baker unhitch the teams and struggle to get the animals out. The wagon is left resting on its axles.

A hasty camp is made. The women cook dinner while the men begin unloading the mired wagon. A squall moves in at dusk and soaks everything. Darkness closes in, damp and cold. The storm moves on, trailing thunderclaps that echo through the mountains. Distant flashes light the night sky.

Baker beds next to Wilson and Fremont under one tarp, while the women and Grandpap bed down under another. As soon as Fremont begins to snore, Wilson nudges Baker. "Baker!" he hisses. "Just so there's no mistaking it, the girl's my intended. I don't want no trouble over her." Baker grunts his assent and wonders what he's gotten himself into.

Up at first light to a thin, blue sky, the men finish unloading the wagon. "We'll make us a corduroy road," instructs Wilson as the men lay out logs and branches for the wheels to ride over. They hitch up the teams, and the four mules pull while the men push. "Give her your shoulders!" shouts Grandpap from the wagon seat as his whip snaps. The wagon rocks in the bog. Slowly, the wheels come out of the mud with a sucking sound and roll up onto the makeshift road.

The men reload the wagon and start up again, with Baker taking over the reins. In less than a mile they come to the top of a steep bluff of forty feet. The wagon tracks disappear over the edge, only to reappear at the bottom. The men stand on the bluff, wondering how to proceed.

"They roped down from this tree," concludes Fremont, standing next to a stout spruce with grooves marking its trunk.

"Then we'll do the same," says Wilson.

They unload the wagons and spend the next two days packing the gear down narrow, grassy ramps. "Don't jostle this powder box, fellas," warns Grandpap, supervising the unloading of his wagon, "or the next party through here will be pickin' up the pieces." The men sweat like mules, even in a cool breeze at over 10,000 feet. By nightfall of the second day, they get it all down. They eat ravenously at the campfire. They all know there's no turning back once the wagons are down. Whatever lies ahead is their fate. Such is their commitment to the new country and to each other.

Grandpap, Margaret and Kate say good night and retire to where their bedding is unrolled between a pair of tall spruce. Wilson yawns and allows that he'll turn in. Baker and Fremont sit up watching the embers glow. Soon, the old muleskinner yawns and heads for the tarp where Wilson is bedded. Baker sits by himself, craving the solitude. He's unaccustomed to traveling with a party, and he feels himself relax while the fire softly pops and flickers. His mind wanders to a girl he knew in Laramie in what seems a different lifetime.

"Mister Baker."

He turns at the whispered sound of his name. Kate looks down on him. She clutches a shawl around her shoulders. Her bedclothes are white by the firelight. Her hair is loose and frames her pretty face in dark waves. Baker gets quickly to his feet. She moves close to him and leans into him, her hands on his chest. She looks up into his face and purses her lips. She leans closer. Her lips brush against his beard. He feels her breath.

Suddenly, the girl spins away, jerked back by Wilson, who flings her to the ground. She lands with a cry of surprise. Wilson leaps at Baker, his hands seeking a hold on his throat. Baker spins from the force of Wilson's weight and both men fall into the fire. The coals burn flesh and hair. Clutched together, they roll free of the flames. Wilson's hands clench at Baker's throat. The man is strong. Baker struggles to work his arms between Wilson's arms, shoving his hands up into Wilson's face. He pushes hard and spreads his elbows, breaking the choke hold. Baker jumps to his feet, his hand instinctively seeking his knife. The blade flashes in the firelight as Wilson struggles to his knees. Baker grips a fistful of Wilson's hair and forces his head back. The tip of the knife blade arcs toward the soft throat, but stops short. Wilson feels the point and ends his struggle. Baker pulls back the knife and brings up his knee hard under Wilson's chin. His teeth clash and he rocks back under the blow. Baker stands over him, the knife in his hand. He is breathing hard, his muscles knotted.

Kate stands frozen on the other side of the fire, her hair in her face, her hands over her mouth. Baker turns to her. "Go!" he orders. She slowly backs away, then turns and disappears. Wilson is dazed. He moans, flat on his back. He slowly props himself up and rubs his jaw. He looks up at Baker's silhouette. "I told you she was mine. You stay away from her or I'll kill you!" seethes Wilson.

"You're readin' somethin' into this that aint there," growls Baker. "Aint nothin' happened."

Wilson scoots back and struggles to his feet. He glares at Baker. "Well...see that it don't happen."

"You be the one to see that it don't!"

Wilson moves back to his bedroll where Fremont is propped up on one elbow, watching. Baker sheathes his knife and gingerly touches a burn on his arm. He massages his throat where Wilson's fingers left imprints. He takes his bedding from beneath the tarp and finds a place under one of the wagons. He sleeps fitfully, incensed both by the girl's impetuosity and Wilson's violent jealousy.

Baker is up at first light checking the mules and taking in the day. Margaret prepares a vat of thick oat porridge sweetened with maple sugar and flavored with currants. Wilson comes late to breakfast. His lower lip is bruised and swollen, and he claims to have bumped into something in the night. The men devour the porridge along with slabs of rich brown bread slathered with raspberry jam. Coffee is a bitter, inky concoction that steams in their cups and softens the bread for swallowing. Margaret reports that Kate is under the weather and assigns Fremont the dish washing detail. The muleskinner grimaces.

After a sullen breakfast, the men push the first wagon into place, backing it up to the edge of the bluff. Wilson takes a long rope and secures it to the whiffletree, then backs away from the bluff, paying out rope from the large coil on his arm. Twice he circles the grooved tree trunk, wrapping the rope. Fremont and Baker secure two shorter ropes to the rear axles to serve as guy lines. Grandpap hovers around the men making sure everything is to his satisfaction.

Wilson gives the word and slowly pays out the long rope as Baker and Fremont push the wagon to the edge of the bluff. Kate arrives with her hair tied back, wearing a gingham dress with a flower print. She sidles toward Wilson. He ignores her and focuses on the wagon. Kate tosses her head and moves back with Margaret, who stands watching from the campfire.

As the wagon teeters at the brink, Fremont and Baker take up the guy lines. Grandpap joins Wilson on the long rope to steady the lowering. Slowly, the wagon tips back, the rear wheels going over the drop. The wraps tighten around the tree, creaking and groaning under the weight of the wagon, but making enough friction to hold the weight. They let out more rope until the wagon dangles vertically against the bluff. Baker and Fremont ply the guy ropes to keep the wagon straight.

"Well, I'll be," says Grandpap, watching the wagon hang in midair. "Never seen anything like it."

Wilson and Grandpap carefully feed out the rope, which rasps around the tree trunk and cuts down into a groove they had notched into a log anchored with pegs at the edge of the bluff. Slowly, the wagon disappears over the edge. Fremont reports the progress of the wagon, which soon settles onto the ground below. They all cheer except for Kate, who sulks by the smoking fire. Baker and Fremont lead the mules down the narrow, grassy ramps and hitch up the wagon, then drive it to where their goods are stacked. They repeat the process with the second wagon, and in several hours, they get everything down in good shape.

Wilson hardly speaks to Baker except in gruff commands. His eyes burn with injury and indignity. Baker knows something has to break or he'll have to leave them. That will mean no pay, and he's in need of some coin in his pocket. It will also mean a sign of guilt where there is no guilt, something contrary to his sense of justice.

It is late afternoon before the wagons are reloaded, and they decide to camp another night before moving further along the ridge. While dinner is underway and Grandpap and Fremont are enjoying their pipes, Baker finds Wilson tending to the teams. Wilson faces him with naked hostility, both fists clenched.

"Wilson, you and me gotta talk, or I leave now. This aint no way to run an outfit."

"Then explain yourself and your intentions," demands Wilson.

"I'm a loner, Wilson. I travel by myself. I aint got no interest in women, surely not in your woman. What happened last night...I didn't have nothin' to do with it. I was just as surprised as you. If I'd 'a felt different about the girl, you wouldn't be standin' there now—and you know that."

Wilson's tension relaxes. His shoulders drop and his fists loosen. He studies Baker. "Well, Baker, I guess I owe you an apology. I'm a little testy trying to get these wagons through. Can you stick it out with us?"

Wilson steps forward and extends a hand. The men shake, their eyes fixed on one another. "You're quick on your feet, Baker. Looks like you got what it takes to make it in this country. Well? Can you stick? I'll make sure the girl keeps her distance."

"I'll stick," says Baker.

That night, before dinner, Wilson makes his play with Kate. He takes her by the hand in the middle of the cooking and, without a word, walks her beyond earshot. The others glance at them as the girl suddenly throws herself at Wilson, her arms around his neck. Grandpap smiles at Margaret, who can't stifle a red blush spreading into her cheeks. "Looks like the boy finally done it," chuckles the patriarch.

In five days they maneuver over two more drops, unloading, lowering the wagons, loading again and moving on. If not for tracks in front of them and the trail breaking that was already done, it would have taken twice the time. "Those first fellas through here had pluck!" muses Grandpap. With careful, plodding progress they cover ten torturous miles in two labor-intensive weeks. That's when the old tracks play out in a maze of bogs and boulder fields, and Baker is unable to scout them out anywhere. "Plum disappeared," he reports at camp.

They push on blindly, coming finally to a steep side hill where they work the wagons down slowly with the mules and keep them upright with guy lines. That evening, from their camp on a narrow bench in the aspen trees, they see the flicker of campfires in the valley a thousand feet below.

While the women are making dinner, Wilson and Baker search for a route down the mountainside through a morass of fallen timber and embedded boulders. They turn around at dark, discouraged, and climb back to the wagons with the last of their strength, their lungs heaving. A big pot of stew is simmering over the fire, and the entire pot is ravenously consumed before a half moon rises, glinting silver through the timber.

The next morning, Wilson and Baker hike down to the mining camp through stands of tall aspens and thickets of thorny brambles. They walk into the camp where men are gathered around a dozen cook fires, each group hailing them with greetings. More camps are scattered among aspen groves along the surging creek. Mules and horses are picketed in the tall grass meadows, but there are no wagons. Theirs will be the first to come into the new camp, loaded with supplies. Wilson approaches a campfire where a man squats before a small canvas tent. The man is bearded and unkempt. Coffee brews in a pot on the coals.

"Lookin' for work?" Wilson queries without introduction.

"I am if y'all are payin' a fair wage?" drawls the tall, lean man, who stands to meet them. His voice gives him away as a Southerner.

"Dollar a day and enough to eat," says Wilson.

The gaunt man studies Wilson and Baker. He shrugs. "Aint doin' nothin' else. What kind 'a work y'all got?"

Half an hour later, Wilson, Baker and the newcomer from Georgia plod slowly up the brushy, timbered hillside. Between gasps for air, the Georgian tells them about the camp of Castle Forks and how a gang of men has formed a company that plans to build a town and a road over the range. He tells them about the camp called Ute City in the valley of the Roaring Fork ten miles down the valley where he says a town company has already cut up the valley into lots and is building a road up to Castle Forks.

At the wagon camp, Jake Sands tells them his tale over a plate of beans and bacon, how he and his partners bushwacked over the Divide from Leadville and bypassed the camps of Independence and Ute City because they heard from a trusted man that Castle Forks would be the next big strike.

"Was he a man named Blodgett?" asks Grandpap.

The Georgian's eyes open wide. "Sure enough was," he says. "You know old Will Blodgett?"

"Yep," says Wilson, "He gave us the same story. That's why we're here."

"Well, me and my partners been here three weeks now and we aint found nothin' yet, but we got our hopes up for a lode." Wilson and Grandpap exchange looks reflecting their own hopes. "This here's big country," says the Georgian, as if answering them, "and we just barely scratched the surface of it."

They set to the task of cutting trees to form a crude path for the wagons. Rather than zigzagging, they decide to go straight down the mountainside. They take the Georgian's advice and chop down several big spruce trees, leaving long branch stubs on the trunks. He instructs them on how to tie the trees to the wagons so they drag as anchors.

Fremont takes the first run, urging the mules on gently and holding hard on the brake while the anchor trees drag along behind, churning up the ground. Baker and Wilson and the Georgian handle guy ropes to keep the wagon from tipping. After two hours of backbreaking work the first wagon reaches the camp at Castle Forks.

Baker takes the reins of the second wagon while the others handle the ropes. Bracing with his legs, he works the brake and feels the trees drag behind him, holding the wagon with jerks and starts. The wagon threatens to tip when one wheel mounts a boulder, but the Georgian holds it back with a guy rope wrapped quickly around a tree. By the time the wagon is safely down, Baker's legs are cramped and stiff. Their exploits have become the center of attention, and the men in camp gather around the wagons. Their furtive eyes look over Margaret and Kate, who are the first of their gender to arrive in Castle Forks, having walked down behind the second wagon. Already men are dickering with Grandpap to trade shares of mine claims for food and supplies.

A big campfire blazes that night and the men of the camp gather to hear the story of crossing the big hill. Grandpap produces a small keg and taps it to raucous cheers. There is excitement in the voices of the men. From those voices boom big plans for a town, a city, wagon roads, railroads, mills, mines, hotels, churches, schools, all to be formed from the raw materials of the new country.

Baker backs slowly away from the fire. He feels strangely out of place here with these men, in this camp, in the wave of excitement they color with such optimism. Instead of catching the fever that swells inside them, Baker feels the need to keep moving. He feels the familiar itch to be in the saddle, to follow game trails, to look across other ridges into other valleys no white man has ever seen. Grandpap and Wilson announce they will continue in the morning to Ute City where they'll throw their dice on the promise of the Roaring Fork. They'll establish a mercantile store and provision prospectors and town builders who will form the foundation for all else to come.

"Baker!" calls out Grandpap, searching the eager faces in the glow of the fire. Dan Baker moves back into the light. "You throwing in your lot with us, Baker?" asks the old man. "You're sure welcome to partner up with us after all we been through."

Baker notices Kate standing next to Wilson, his arm around her shoulders. Wilson's made his claim and he wants all the men in camp to know it. Baker glances at Grandpap and Margaret, steadfast by the fire. His gaze passes over the men, rough and ready men searching for something, always searching. Wilson and the others will make out fine, Baker figures, but their life is not his. This is where their paths divide.

"I reckon I'll move on," states Baker.

"Where to?" queries Wilson.

"Over another hill, I guess. There's always a bigger hill, aint there?"

Wilson leaves Kate's side. He moves around the fire glow and stands before Baker, a look of triumph in his eyes. "Good luck to you, Baker, on the biggest hill you can find." They shake hands. Wilson slaps him on the back.

"Here. You might be needin' this," says Grandpap. He tosses a leather purse, heavy with coins. The purse arcs over the sparking fire, and Baker catches it. "You earned it," says the old man.

"Much obliged," says Baker.

The next morning the grasses are white with frost. There's a bite to the air. Dan Baker is saddled and ready to ride down the valley to see what Ute City is all about. He walks his saddle horse, with the packhorse tethered behind, to the fire ring where Fremont squats, a bulge of tobacco in his cheek. Baker gives a salute to the muleskinner. Fremont touches his rebel cap and lets loose a spray of juice into the embers. A loud hiss sends up a white puff of steam.

"You take it easy, Fremont," says Baker.

"I'll take it whatever way I can," utters the old man with a wink.

Dan Baker swings up into the saddle and nudges the buckskin's flanks. Fremont watches as he slowly threads his way through the tall willows, the packhorse in tow. Fremont returns his gaze to the fire. He squirts another stream of tobacco juice onto the flames, sending a pungent plume into the cool, clear mountain air. ☆

OTHER BOOKS
BY PAUL ANDERSEN

Aspen: Rocky Mountain Paradise, 2010
Aspen's Rugged Splendor, 2007
Power in the Mountains, 2002
East of Aspen, 2000
Aspen: Body, Mind and Spirit, 1999
Elk Mountains Odyssey, 1998
Aspen: Portrait of a Rocky Mountain Town, 1992
Aspen in Color, 1990